Back [...]

A collector's edition of favorite titles from one of the world's best-loved romance authors. Harlequin is proud to bring back these sought-after titles and present them as one cherished collection.

BETTY NEELS:
COLLECTOR'S EDITION

HARLEQUIN®

Betty Neels spent her childhood and youth in Devonshire before training as a nurse and midwife. She was an army nursing sister during the war, married a Dutchman and subsequently lived in Holland for fourteen years. She now lives with her husband in Dorset, and has a daughter and grandson. Her hobbies are reading, animals, old buildings and, of course, writing. Betty started to write on retirement from nursing, incited by a lady in a library bemoaning the lack of romantic novels.

Mrs. Neels is always delighted to receive fan letters, but would truly appreciate it if they could be directed to Harlequin Mills & Boon Ltd., 18-24 Paradise Road, Richmond, Surrey, TW9 1SR, England.

Books by Betty Neels

BETTY NEELS

PINEAPPLE GIRL

COLLECTOR'S EDITION

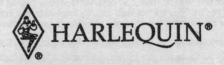

HARLEQUIN®

TORONTO • NEW YORK • LONDON
AMSTERDAM • PARIS • SYDNEY • HAMBURG
STOCKHOLM • ATHENS • TOKYO • MILAN • MADRID
PRAGUE • WARSAW • BUDAPEST • AUCKLAND

ISBN 0-373-63105-7

PINEAPPLE GIRL

First North American Publication 1999.

Copyright © 1977 by Betty Neels.

CHAPTER ONE

THE WARD was in twilight, the patients settling
down for the night, those recently operated upon
already sedated and made as comfortable as possible, while those ladies who were once more on
their legs were putting in the last hair rollers, clean-
ing their teeth, and drinking the final dregs of the
cocoa or Horlick's which the junior night nurse
had been handing round. There were curtains
round the bed by the door, though, and everyone
was careful not to look in that direction. Mrs
Peake, who had been in the ward for weeks now,
was about to leave it. She had been quiet and un-
complaining and grateful for even the smallest service, and as Miss Crow, a convalescent appendix,
remarked: 'It did seem 'ard to 'ave ter die all quiet-
like.' Her listeners had nodded in agreement and
one of them had whispered: 'Yer so right, dearie,
but at least she's got our nice Staff with 'er.'

There was another round of whispered agreement. Eloise Bennett was liked by all her patients;
she somehow managed to make a long night
shorter, and the coming of morning something
pleasant, even for those due for theatre that day.

And she was a good nurse, too, seeing to uncomfortable pillows before the bed's occupant had time to complain, whisking sheets smooth, knowing when to be firm and when to sympathise, and over and above these things, she knew her work well— all the complications of drips and pumps, ventilators and tubes held no fears for her; sudden emergencies were dealt with with a calm born of experience and common sense, so that although she had only been qualified for a little more than a year, she had already been singled out by authority to be thrust into Sister's blue the moment a vacancy occurred.

She came from behind the curtains now, a tall girl, with a splendid figure and a wealth of nut-brown hair piled under her nurse's cap, and a face which could be considered plain but for a pair of large hazel eyes, richly fringed, for her nose was too short and her mouth far too wide and her brows, although nicely arched, were dark and thick. She smiled as she encountered the gaze of the little group of women still out of their beds, said in a pleasant voice: 'Ladies, you're missing your beauty sleep,' and went past them to start her evening round at the top of the ward.

The first three beds offered no hindrance to her progress; operation cases of that afternoon, they were already settled for the night and sleeping, so she merely checked their conditions, studied their charts and moved on down the ward. Old Mrs James was in the next bed, elderly and crotchety and impatient of the major surgery she had undergone a few days previously; Eloise stayed with her for a few minutes, listened to her small grievances, promised sleeping pills very shortly and went on to the next bed.

The ward was almost full, only one empty bed at the end of the row stood ready to receive any emergency which might arrive at a moment's notice. It would have to be moved presently, thought Eloise as she sped past it, for if anyone came in during the night the whole ward would be awakened by the trundling of the trolley down its length. She sighed a little, for the day staff could have done it easily without disturbing anyone at all...

The first bed on the other side of the ward still had its overhead light on, its occupant sitting up against her pillows, reading. The new patient, admitted that day for operation in the morning and according to the day nurses, as tiresome a woman as one could wish not to meet. Eloise stopped by the bed, said, 'Good evening, Mrs Fellows,' in her nice quiet voice and pointed out that bed lights had been due out ten minutes earlier. 'I'm going to give you something to make you sleep,' she promised. 'You've had a drink, haven't you? Nurse will bring you a cup of tea early in the morning and get you ready for theatre.'

Mrs Fellows was aggressively blonde, extremely fat and far from sweet-tempered. 'And who are you?' she wanted to know, belligerently. 'I shan't sleep a wink, no one knows how I suffer with my poor nerves—the least sound and I wake. I need the greatest care and attention—the very thought of my operation makes me feel faint!'

Eloise considered privately that fainting was the last thing that Mrs Fellows was likely to do; shout, scream, wake everyone up—yes, very probably; anything to focus attention on her plump person.

'Don't think about it,' she advised, 'there's no need, you know, because you'll know absolutely nothing about it...'

Mrs Fellows shot her a look of dislike. 'Easy to talk,' she sneered, 'a great hulking girl like you, as hard as nails and never a day's illness. You're all alike,' she added vaguely.

'I expect we seem like that to you,' conceded Eloise, 'but we're not really.' She stretched up and turned off the bed light. 'I'll be back presently with those pills.' She smiled kindly at the tiresome woman and turned to the occupant of the next bed, Mrs White, a small, wiry woman who was going home the next day and who greeted her with a smile. 'I'll miss yer, dearie,' she said softly. 'It'll be nice to get 'ome, but I'll miss yer... 'Ere, this is from me old man and me. Yer been an angel and we wants yer ter 'ave it.'

And Mrs White, with a swift movement worthy of a magician, heaved at something under the blankets and produced a pineapple.

'Oh!' said Eloise, startled, and then: 'Mrs White, what a simply lovely present—thank you, and your husband. I've—I've never had such a delightful surprise.' She clasped the fruit to her person and bent to kiss the donor. She was going to look a little strange finishing the round hugging it to her aproned bosom, but to do anything else would hurt Mrs White's feelings. She tucked it under one arm, where it got dreadfully in the way, until she was back at her desk once more, where she put it in a prominent position, mindful of her patient's watchful eye.

It stayed there for the rest of the night, while Eloise, with her junior trotting beside her, dealt with all the small emergencies which cropped up. She dealt with the inevitable admission too, a young girl who had got involved in a fight between her boy-friend and some other young man; she had been punched and knocked around and both hands had been cut where she had tried to take the knife away from one of them. She was still shocked when she was admitted; Eloise dealt with her gently, sedated her under the eye of the house surgeon on duty, and went back to her routine chores; they had to be fitted in however many times she was interrupted. And the girl was quiet, which was more than could be said for the two men admitted with her. Lucy Page, the staff nurse on Men's Surgical, had a good deal to say about them when she got down to her meal.

'A nasty pair,' she informed Eloise. 'I've got them in the two-bedded ward opposite the office—they're laid low at the moment and there's a member of the force with them, thank heaven, but I don't envy the day staff. How's yours?'

Eloise told her, gobbling rice pudding, her mind already hours ahead, working out how she could best catch up with the night's work before the morning was upon her. 'Someone gave me a pineapple,' she informed the table at large, and added apologetically: 'I would have brought it down with me, but I thought it would have been nice to take home...'

There was a chorus of assent; everyone there knew that Eloise lived in a poky little flat behind the Imperial War Museum—true, it was on the fringe of a quite respectable middle-class district, but with, as it were, an undesirable neighbourhood breathing down its neck. It had been all that her mother could afford after her father had died, and now, several years later, they both knew that she had made a mistake, giving up their pretty little house in the Somerset village and coming to live in an alien London. At the time it had seemed a good idea; Eloise had just started her training as a nurse, and if she lived with her mother there would be more money to eke out Mrs Bennett's tiny pension, and if her mother had stayed in Eddlescombe, then Eloise would have been hard put to it to find the fare home, even for an occasional visit.

Accordingly, when her sister-in-law had suggested that she might be able to find them a flat near St Goth's, Mrs Bennett had been delighted. Surprised too; her elder brother's wife and now widow had never liked them overmuch; she had paid an occasional visit, turning up her long nose at the smallness of the village house, sneering at the small country pleasures they enjoyed, wondering, out loud and in a penetrating voice, how they could exist without central heating, colour TV and the amenities of town life. But after Mr Bennett's funeral she had stayed on for a few days, full of suggestions as to their future. And at the time they had been grateful, for it had seemed a way out of their difficulties, but now, sadly, with the wisdom of hindsight they knew that they had made a mistake.

Mrs Bennett had never settled in London and

although they lived more comfortably now that Eloise was trained and had more money, it was still hard to make ends meet. Besides, her aunt, now that her first enthusiastic efforts had palled and she had seen them settled in their new home, had rather washed her hands of them, not that Mrs Bennett would have accepted any help from her. A small, rather timid woman, sheltered all her married life by her husband and then by his daughter, she had nonetheless a good deal of pride which made it unthinkable to rely on any form of charity, especially from her sister-in-law, so she lived uncomplainingly in the hideous block of flats, her treasured furniture around her, and looked upon with good-humoured tolerance and casual affection by her neighbours, while she, for her part, was ever ready to babysit, read aloud to the bedbound and offer a ready hand when it was needed.

Eloise hated it too, but the hate hadn't soured her. She had done well during her training, been the gold medallist for her year and was well on the way to a Sister's post—Junior Night Sister first, the stepping off point for promotion, and then the chance of a ward of her own—and when that happened, and it wouldn't be all that long to wait, she had made up her mind to find a home for them both, in or near Eddlescombe. She would be earning enough to do that, and although she would hate living in the hospital, she would be able to go home fairly often and at least have the satisfaction of knowing that her mother was happy.

She was thinking about it as she went off duty in the morning after a tiring night, culminating in Mrs Fellows' shocking behaviour when she had wakened at six o'clock. Little Mrs Peake had died in the early hours of the morning, as gently and quietly as she had lived, and Eloise and her nurse had done what they had to do in a sad silence, for there had been no one to mourn the dear soul; as far as anyone knew she had no family and very few friends. They made up the bed with silent speed and went back to their endless little jobs until the first of the operation cases woke, to be instantly made comfortable for the day, sat up, given a drink, and where necessary, another injection. They had all the poorly ones settled by the time the rest of the ward roused itself and the mobile patients began their self-appointed task of handing round the early tea.

It was in the middle of this cheerful bustle that Mrs Fellows had made herself heard; she refused in no uncertain manner to drink her tea, take a bath and put on her theatre gown; she had refused loudly, rudely and at great length, so that Eloise, called from the re-packing of dressings, changing of drips and filling in charts, was hard put to keep her patience and temper—something Mrs Fellows' neighbours didn't do. She was told to belt up, shut up and invited to buzz off, their advice given in the pungent, forceful language of the cockney, with strong recommendations to mind what she said to Staff. 'For yer don't know yer luck,' declared one old lady, still without her teeth but none the less a force to be reckoned with. 'She's a h'angel, she is, an' yer jist wait till ternight, yer won't 'arf be glad she's 'ere ter look after yer.'

The chorus of agreement was uttered in so menacing a tone that Eloise had intervened, begging everyone in a calm voice to hush a little: 'Don't forget the ladies at the other end,' she reminded her belligerent supporters, 'they're not feeling too bright and most of them have just had injections.'

She had pulled the curtains round Mrs Fellows' bed then, while that lady muttered abuse at her. It would have been nice, she thought tiredly, if she could have muttered back at her; the night had been a heavy one and she was dog-tired, and going off duty presently, with the prospect of a lot more of Mrs Fellows when she came on again that night, did nothing to cheer her. She had sent her junior nurse on ahead while she went back to say a final farewell to Mrs White, and then, with her bag, bulging with the knitting she hadn't had a chance to do, and the pineapple clasped under one arm, she had set off for the canteen, a vast, dreary place in the basement.

Women's Surgical was on the second floor and nurses were supposed to use the stairs; in any case both lifts were in use. Eloise started off running down the stone steps, late and tired and a little cross. She had reached the ground floor and had begun to traverse the back lobby in order to reach the last, narrow flight of stairs, when she saw Sir Arthur Newman, the senior consultant on the surgical side, standing directly below the staircase she was tearing down, looking the other way, talking to a tall man with very broad shoulders, facing her. The man was good-looking—very, noted her tired eye, with fair hair and commanding features—and he was staring at her.

And no wonder, she thought peevishly; her hair was coming loose from its bun and her cape was hanging from one shoulder; all the same, he didn't have to look at her as though she were surrounded by winking lights or something. She frowned and lifted her chin because he had begun to smile a little, and that was a great pity, because she took a step which wasn't there and fell flat on her face. The knitting cushioned her fall, but the pineapple bounded ahead and landed with a squashy thump on the man's shoe, denting itself nastily.

The shoe's wearer kicked it gently to one side,

surveyed his large, well-shod foot and bent to pick her up. The pair of them hauled her to her feet rather as though she had been a sack of coals, dusted her down with kindly hands and while Sir Arthur handed her her knitting, his companion bent to pick up the crushed fruit.

'So sorry,' said Eloise breathlessly, 'very clumsy of me...' Her eye fell on the pineapple and her face dropped. 'Oh, it's spoilt!' She lifted a worried face to his. 'And I did so want to...' She paused; this stranger wouldn't be in the least interested in her intentions regarding her gift. 'I hope it didn't hurt your foot,' she said politely.

'I have large feet,' he had a slow, pleasantly deep voice, 'and there's no harm done—only to this.' He handed over the battered thing. 'A present?' he inquired gently.

'Well, yes—you know, someone going home... so kind...thank you both very much...breakfast...I'm late...' She smiled at them both, happily forgetful of her deplorable appearance, and nipped across the lobby and down the stairs, to be greeted by her friends wanting to know why she was so late and had someone dragged her through a hedge backwards.

She sat down with her plate of porridge and showered it with sugar. 'Well, I got off late, and then I fell down in the back lobby and Sir Arthur was there and picked me up.' For some reason she didn't want to tell them about the man who had been with him. 'I've ruined my pineapple, though.'

'Put it in the fridge,' someone suggested. 'Perhaps it'll harden up—you've got nights off after tonight, haven't you?'

Eloise fetched scrambled eggs on toast and began to devour them. 'And three weeks' holiday only two weeks away.'

'What will you do?'

'Stay at home—I expect we'll go out, exhibitions and things,' she observed vaguely; London at the beginning of October wasn't really the place for a holiday. Now, Eddlescombe would be lovely; bonfires in the gardens and falling leaves and long walks under an autumn sky... She pushed aside the rest of her breakfast, no longer hungry, and got herself another cup of tea. 'Does anyone want any stamps?' she asked. 'I've got to go to the post office on the way home.'

She went home by bike, on an ancient machine which creaked and groaned through the morning traffic and brought her finally to the block of flats where she and her mother lived. The building looked bleaker than usual as she wheeled it to the basement shelter and chained it up for the day before walking up two flights of stairs to the second floor, the pineapple, very much the worse for wear, secure on top of the knitting in her bag. It looked a bit second-hand by now, but at least most of it would be edible.

Second-hand or not, Mrs Bennett was delighted with it, making light of the damage. 'What a lovely surprise,' she declared happily. 'We'll have it at supper.' Her still pretty face creased into a ready smile, while her eyes, hazel like her daughter's, noted the tired white face.

'A bad night, love? Well, only two more nights before you get nights off—what shall we do with them? There's that exhibition of pottery—oh, and your aunt wants to come and see us…'

Eloise had cast off her outdoor uniform and was putting on the kettle. 'Oh, Mother, must she? She only comes when she wants something.'

'Yes, I know, darling, but this time she's bringing Deborah Pringle with her—remember I knew her years ago and we were always great friends—still are in a way, for we write regularly even though she doesn't live in England. I should like to see her again.'

She went back into the kitchen and made the tea and they went into the sitting room, small and rather crowded with the furniture they had brought with them from Somerset; all the same, it was a pretty room with a few flowers and some small pieces of silver on the sideboard. The pair of them sat down by the window and drank their tea and presently Eloise went off to have her bath and go to bed. Really, night duty was no life at all, she thought sleepily as she brushed her hair; here it was almost eleven o'clock and she would have to be up soon after five so that she could eat her supper in peace before going back on duty—there was no time to read or talk. 'Poor Mother,' she muttered, 'it's even worse for her.'

She went to say goodnight to her parent, busy in the kitchen, and then retired to take her night's rest in her topsy-turvy world. It had been a horrid night, she reflected gloomily as she curled up in bed. At least, not quite horrid, for there had been that nice man… She fell asleep thinking about him.

Her mother called her, as she always did, with a cup of tea and sat on the end of the bed while she drank it. 'You've not slept very much, have you?' she wanted to know.

'Well, once the children get out of school…' Eloise tried to sound cheerful because she knew that her mother worried about her wakefulness, and her mother nodded and went on:

'That pineapple, dear—was there something special about it?'

'Just a pineapple, Mother.'

'Yes, I know that—but a special delivery man called after lunch with a Fortnum and Mason basket, I opened it because all the man said was "name of Bennett", the way they always do—and it's crammed with fruit: three pineapples and grapes and those enormous pears and apples...there's a note.'

She handed an envelope to her daughter and didn't say a word while Eloise opened it and read the brief note inside: 'Allow me to offer compensation for the damage done by my foot this morning.' The signature was unintelligible and it was addressed to the Pineapple Girl.

'Well!' said Eloise, and then: 'He must be nuts.'

'Who, dear?' Mrs Bennett's voice was casual, masking her seething curiosity.

'Well, there was this man...' Eloise related the morning's happening without trimmings. 'And my hair was coming down—I looked a perfect fright—you know...' She paused. 'Mother, have I ever reminded you of a pineapple?'

Her mother took the question seriously. 'No, dear. You're not a beauty, but you're not knobbly—your hair grows very prettily too, not out of the top of your head.'

'How did he know where I lived?'

'He only had to ask, presumably. Porters, or someone,' said Mrs Bennett vaguely. 'If he was talking to Sir Arthur Newman he must have been respectable, so of course they would have told him.'

Eloise looked at her mother with loving amusement. 'Yes, well…' She finished her tea and went along to the sitting room where the basket was displayed on the table. It was indeed a splendid sight, Eloise walked all round it, eyeing its contents. 'I can't thank him,' she observed at length. 'I haven't a clue who he is, have I? I could ask, I suppose, but I don't think I want to—I mean if—if he'd wanted to see me again he would have put an address or said so.' She glanced at her mother and said seriously: 'He was a very handsome man, he'd hardly lower his sights to me, you know. I expect he just felt sorry.'

She sighed; usually she didn't waste time pining for a beautiful face, but just for a moment she wanted most desperately to be absolutely eye-catching. 'Oh, well,' she said at length, and then: 'We've got enough fruit to open a shop, isn't it marvellous?'

It seemed only fair to take Mrs White's gift back on duty that evening, to be shared among her friends at their midnight dinner; it made a nice change from the creamed rice and jellied fruit which were on the menu night after night. But Eloise didn't get any herself; she got down late to her meal because Mrs Fellows had made the early part

of the night hideous with her loud moans and com-
plaints. She had been sedated early because the day
staff had been hindered in their evening's work by
her constant demands for this, that and the other
thing, but that had worn off by ten o'clock, and
although Eloise got the house surgeon on duty to
come and look at her and write her up for further
sedation, he had told her to wait until midnight
before giving it.

'She's not in pain,' he declared, 'just determined
to make life hell for everyone else—let's see, supposing we give her...' He wrote busily. 'That
should keep her quiet until morning and you can
repeat it at six o'clock if she's still rampaging.' He
thrust the chart at Eloise. 'It was only an EUA,
after all...not even surgery.'

Cycling home in the morning, Eloise reflected
that the night had been awful—thank heaven there
was only one more to go before her nights off.

And that night was so madly busy that she had
no time for her own thoughts at all; with operation
cases to settle, two severe accident cases to admit,
an emergency case for the theatre at two o'clock
in the morning, and Mrs Fellows, due home in the
morning, but still complaining loudly, adding her
quota to the night's bedlam. Eloise, too tired to
know whether she was coming or going, ate her

breakfast in a trance, got herself home and fell into her bed after a quick cup of tea and a hot bath.

She had six nights off due to her and it was on the third of these that Mrs Bennett's visitors came. Her sister-in-law arrived first; a tall, commanding woman with a penetrating voice and cold good looks, she pecked at their cheeks, told them that they both looked tired, chose a chair with deliberation and loosened the expensive furs she was wearing. Watching her aunt, Eloise found herself wondering how she had come to marry her father's elder brother in the first place, although perhaps it wasn't so strange, as he had been successful; making money as easily as a good cook makes pastry, quite unlike her own father, content to work in his book shop, specializing in rare books and engravings. That he had loved herself and her mother she had no doubt, but books were his real love and he had lived largely in a world of his own far removed from the more mundane life around him. Which had probably accounted for the fact that when he died very suddenly from a coronary, it was discovered that his insurances had lapsed for a number of years and that he had mortgaged the shop and house in order to find the money to buy the rare books he had coveted. As a consequence he had left his wife and daughter very ill provided for and although neither of them had blamed him in the slightest for this, his sister-in-law had never ceased, on every possible occasion, to mention his improvidence.

The lady made just such a remark now, once she had settled herself, and went on in her bossy way: 'You need a change, both of you, and I have the solution.'

She held up a beringed hand to stop any questioning, although neither of her listeners had had any intention of speaking; they had long ago decided that the only way to treat their overbearing relation was to give every appearance of attention and then go their own way, but the lady went on, just as though she had received a gratifying murmur of admiration: 'But I shall say no more until Deborah Pringle arrives.' She frowned and glanced at her watch. 'She should be here now.'

As though Mrs Pringle had been given her cue, the doorbell rang and Eloise went to answer it. She had met Mrs Pringle a number of times and liked her; she was a small bustling creature with a kindly nature which never sought to boss others around and Eloise had often wondered how she had come to be a friend of her aunt's. She came in now, exclaiming cheerfully, 'I'm a little late, but the taxi couldn't find you and I'm hopeless at telling people how to get to places.' She gave Eloise a kiss and added warmly: 'Your lovely hair—how I do envy you, my dear. How's your mother?'

Eloise said dryly: 'Aunt says she needs a holiday…'

'And I daresay she does but she's not one to waste time pining for something—not if I know her, and I should do after all these years.' She smiled widely and whispered: 'What's the betting that I'm wearing the wrong kind of hat?'

She was greeted with pleasure by Mrs Bennett and more austerely by that lady's sister-in-law, who, sure enough, told her at once: 'That's not the hat for you, Deborah—far too young…'

'But I feel young.' Mrs Pringle sat down between her two friends and looked at them in turn, rather like a referee might look at two boxers before a fight. She said cheerfully: 'Well, Mary, it's delightful to see you again—a pity I don't come to England more often and when I do, it's almost impossible to get away; Cor likes me to be with him all the time.'

'He's not with you this time?' asked Mrs Bennett.

'He went back last week—simply had to…' And when her friend cast her an inquiring look: 'I wasn't allowed to travel; I came over here for an operation, nothing vital, but I have to stay for a check-up before I go home.' She changed the conversation then, and it wasn't until Eloise had fetched the tea and they had finished the sandwiches and home made cake that she reverted to herself.

'I've a favour to ask,' she began a shade diffidently. 'You see, I met Maggie a short while ago,' she paused to smile at that forbidding lady, 'and I mentioned that I was going back home in a short time and wanted to take a nurse with me, just for a little while, you know, and so she telephoned you, Mary, meaning to ask if Eloise was free, and you told her that she had a holiday in a couple of weeks. Now that would be simply splendid if only she would agree to come with me.' She flashed a smile at Eloise. 'Nothing much to do, just a small dressing and my temperature and so on, and I promise her that she shall have plenty of time to do what she likes.'

Eloise found her astonished voice. 'How kind of you to think of me,' she exclaimed, 'but you see I can't leave Mother alone...'

'Ah,' Mrs Pringle beamed in mild triumph, 'it just so happens in the most extraordinary way imaginable that I met Mrs Plunkett last week— remember her at Eddlescombe? Well, she was asking about you, Mary, and said how much she would like to see you again and if only you were on your own she would love to have you to stay—

you know she has only that dear little cottage with two bedrooms?' She paused and looked around her. Mrs Bennett was staring at her with rapt attention, Eloise's nice, ordinary face betrayed her suspicion that the whole thing was a put up job and her aunt looked vaguely irritated as she always did when someone else was doing the talking.

'I know it sounds too good to be true,' declared Mrs Pringle with a glance at Eloise, 'but that's exactly what happened, and I thought how marvellous it would be if Eloise were to come with me and you, Mary, could go and stay with Beryl Plunkett. What do you say?'

Eloise darted a quick look at the longing on her mother's face. 'I think it's a super idea, Mrs Pringle; I'd love to look after you, and if Mother's with Mrs Plunkett I should be quite happy about going. What do you think, Mother?'

Mrs Bennett smiled widely at no one in particular. 'Well, darling, it does sound delightful, but you're sure you...you'll have a lovely time... Eddlescombe will be heavenly at this time of year...'

Mrs Pringle smiled too. 'Then that's settled. Eloise, when does your holiday start? I planned to go down to say goodbye to Beryl. You could drive down with me, Mary, and I'll come back and collect Eloise on the following day.'

Mrs Bennett looked overwhelmed. 'You're re-

ally going down to Eddlescombe? It would be
lovely to drive down with you—if Eloise could
manage for a couple of days?'

'Easily, darling.' Eloise smiled at her mother.
She hadn't seen that look on her face for a long
time; even if she hadn't wanted to go with Mrs
Pringle, she would have declared her delight at the
prospect—and she did want to go, not only because it would give her mother the chance of a
holiday; it would be fun to go somewhere different.
Which reminded her. 'You know, I'm not at all
sure where you live,' she told Mrs Pringle.

'Holland, my dear. We've lived all over the
world, you know, but now Cor is permanently
based there, and he being a Dutchman finds that
very satisfactory—so do I; we live in Groningen,
in the north and within easy reach of the city.
There's a car if you care to drive it, and the country
around us is delightful—quiet but not isolated. Cor
is away a good deal, but he's always home at
weekends and we have friends—I think you might
like it.' She caught the questioning look in Eloise's
eye and added: 'I'll tell you about myself later;
one's little illnesses are always so boring for other
people.'

She turned back to Mrs Bennett. 'That's settled,
then, and how very pleased I am. Shall I collect
you in—two weeks, is it? We'll fix the exact day

later—and Eloise will be free the day after you go to Eddlescombe, won't she? Nothing could be better.' She gathered up her gloves and handbag. 'I really must fly—can I give you a lift, Maggie?'

She so obviously expected her offer to be accepted that Eloise's aunt got to her feet quite quickly and with unusual meekness, and it was during their rather protracted farewells that Mrs Pringle said quietly to Eloise: 'You're back on duty in two days, aren't you? Could you manage to meet me one morning before you come home?'

There was no time to ask questions. Eloise said yes and named a day and time and wondered what she was going to be told, for obviously Mrs Pringle was going to tell her something; something which she didn't care to discuss with everyone; something to do with her op. Eloise reviewed her surgery and decided that it was probably a good deal more serious than Mrs Pringle had implied.

It was; sitting in the visitors' room in the Nurses' Home after breakfast a few mornings later, her visit disclosed quite simply that she had inoperable cancer; that there was little more to be done and that she and her husband had decided that she should return to Groningen and live out the rest of her life among her friends and in the home she loved. 'I have a simply splendid doctor,' she told Eloise cheerfully. 'It was he who sent me to Sir

Arthur Newman in the first place—you've worked
for him, haven't you, dear? I was in a nursing
home, of course, though I should have been just as
happy in hospital, but Cor insisted, bless him...'
She smiled. 'So now you know—or did you
guess?'

'Almost—I thought it might be more serious
than you wanted us to think, and when you mentioned a dressing...'

'And you really don't mind coming? It's silly of
me, I know, but I have to get used to the idea and
I thought if I had someone I knew with me, just
for a little while, then I can face it. They tell me I
can expect six months, perhaps a little longer.'

Eloise got out of her chair and went to kneel by
her visitor. 'You're brave, Mrs Pringle, and I'll do
all I can to help you. Your husband must be very
upset.'

'Poor dear, he is. Do you believe in miracles,
Eloise?'

'Yes, and I think most nurses and doctors do;
you see, now and then there is a miracle, and who
knows, it might be yours.'

Her visitor smiled crookedly. 'Bless you for saying that! I believe we're going to get on very well
together.' She got to her feet. 'Not a word to your
mother, mind—no one knows, only you and Cor
and Sir Arthur, and of course my own doctor.'

'Dutch?' asked Eloise.

'From Groningen.' Mrs Pringle looked vaguely speculative for a moment. 'I expect you'll get on well with each other; he's a mild sort of man. Now I'm going for you have to go home and go to bed. Will you tell your mother that I'll write to her within the next day or so? And I'll let you know at what time I'll call for you.' She leaned up and kissed Eloise's cheek. 'You're a dear girl.'

Eloise cycled home thoughtfully, only half her mind on the traffic. Mrs Pringle was indeed a brave woman, and the idea of leaving her alone again after a couple of weeks went against the grain. She frowned over the problem until she was brought back to the present by a bus driver alongside her, waiting at the traffic lights, asking her from his cab if she had taken root. He said it nicely, for she was in uniform, but it recalled her to her whereabouts. She made haste home after that and spent the next hour or so listening to her mother's delighted comments on her forthcoming holiday. 'I am looking forward to it,' declared Mrs Bennett for the hundredth time, 'and I only hope you'll enjoy yourself too, darling.'

Eloise gave her mother a hug. 'I shall enjoy every minute of it,' she assured her, reflecting that to do anything else wouldn't help Mrs Pringle at all. 'And now I'm off to bed, darling—I had a beastly night.'

CHAPTER TWO

THE FORTNIGHT went very quickly. The ward was busy for one thing, and for another, both Eloise and her mother had something to plan for. Refuting that wise but cautious saying about rainy days, Eloise took her mother shopping and persuaded her parent to invest in a good tweed suit, pointing out with rather muddled good sense that the garment in question would probably be twice the price by the time they could afford to buy it. Mrs Bennett, thus spurred on, found a dear little hat to go with it, had her good shoes re-soled and then turned her attention to her daughter. Eloise dressed well, considering she did so on a minuscule amount of money, but as her mother pointed out, Mrs Pringle very likely lived in some style, and she had to admit that her winter coat, although well cut and nicely fitting, was now about to see its third winter—moreover, she was heartily sick of it; something would have to be done to liven it up. This they achieved at a reasonable outlay by the purchase of an angora cap, scarf and gloves in a warm shade of honey which helped the dark brown of the coat considerably.

Eloise found a dress too of almost the same shade; one of dozens similar in Marks and Spencer, but as she pointed out, the chance of anyone in Holland knowing that was remote. It was simply cut, with long sleeves and a wide belt to define her small waist, and if the occasion warranted she would dress it up with a neck scarf or some beads. Sweaters she already had, and skirts and an elderly velvet dress the colour of a mole, bought in their more affluent days; no longer high fashion, but it would, at a pinch, pass muster. The two ladies went home, packed their cases and professed themselves well pleased with their purchases.

It had been arranged that Mrs Bennett should be fetched by Mrs Pringle's car—a hired one, and as she confided to Eloise, it would be a treat in itself just to be driven all the way to Somerset. 'Though Deborah always drove herself,' she remarked, 'and when I asked her why she had a chauffeur she said something about it being not like the old days and there was too much traffic. I must say I was quite surprised.' Which Eloise wasn't.

Her mother gone, Eloise combated loneliness with a great deal of housework, slept soundly and went on duty for the last time before her holiday. The tiresome Mrs Fellows had long since gone, but the ward was full and some of the patients were ill; she went off duty tired out and with the good-natured wishes of her friends ringing in her ears she cycled home, thankful that she had nothing to do but go to bed. She got up early, finished her packing, cooked herself an early supper, washed her hair and after touring the little flat to make sure that everything was in apple pie order, went back to bed again; she would have to be up in good time in the morning, as she was to be fetched at eight o'clock.

She woke to a bright day, the chilliness of autumn masked by brilliant sunshine. The winter coat was going to be a little heavy, but worn without a hat it would have to do. She took extra care with her pretty hair, made up her face carefully, collected her passport and purse, went through her handbag once more, and sat down to wait.

Mrs Pringle was on time; Eloise saw the car from the window, gave a final look round and went downstairs. She felt excited now and happier than she had been for a long time, although she knew that the happiness would be dimmed before long— Mrs Pringle had put a brave face on things, but there were going to be days when she wouldn't feel so good, when Eloise would have to coax and encourage and somehow rekindle the spark of hope every patient had tucked away inside them. And there was always the possibility, however remote, that Mrs Pringle might make a recovery—it could happen, no one knew why, and it didn't happen often, but it was something to bear in mind and work for.

Her patient was in the back of the car; if she were secretly worried about herself, no trace of it showed on her face. She told the driver to stow the luggage in the boot, invited Eloise to get in beside her and exclaimed happily: 'I'm so thrilled at the idea of going home! I've been thinking of some of the things we might do together, but first I must tell you about your mother. I left her looking ten years younger and so happy—she sent her love and said you were to enjoy yourself. Such a dear creature and not changed at all, which is more than I can say for your aunt—how lucky she is to have you, Eloise. I always wanted a daughter. Of course it's lovely having Pieter, but he doesn't live at home.' She sighed. 'We always said that we would have six children.'

'Mother wanted a large family...'

'Yes. Ah, well, perhaps when you marry you'll make up for it and have a pack of them—that will please her, though it's not fashionable.'

'Pooh,' declared Eloise, 'who cares about fashion?' and just for a moment she saw herself, surrounded by several quite beautiful children, with a pleasant house in the background and an enormous garden, and somewhere close by, but regrettably vague, a husband. She might have elaborated on his appearance, only her companion was speaking again.

'We'll be met at Schiphol—Cor will be there with the car—this one is hired; as you know. It won't take long to drive home from there—it's less than a hundred and fifty miles. The village where we live is called Scharmerbloem—it's small, but then you like the country, don't you, dear? Just a few houses and a church. Groningen is only ten miles away, though.'

'And your doctor—does he live in Groningen?'

'Well, he has his consulting rooms there and beds in the hospital, but he lives quite close by us, by the side of a charming lake called Schildermeer. The village is called Oostersum—it's as small as ours.' She paused. 'We do depend on our cars, of course, as although the main road isn't too far away, it's a good walk, though once you're there the bus service is good.'

They were threading their way through the London traffic towards the airport and Mrs Pringle glanced out of the window rather wistfully so that Eloise said quickly: 'Of course you'll be coming back in a month or so for a check-up, won't you? Sir Arthur would want that.'

'Yes, although he did suggest that he might

come and see me—he's an old friend of our doctor and it would give him an excuse to visit him.'

'What a good idea! I expect your doctor knows everything there is to know about you, Mrs Pringle?'

'Yes, dear, and I've great faith in him; he's quiet and solid and sure of himself.'

Eloise decided silently that probably he was big-headed; quite likely he wouldn't take kindly to giving instructions to a foreign nurse. It was to be hoped that his English was adequate. She reflected uneasily that she had better get herself a dictionary and learn a few vital words of the Dutch language. In a way it was a pity that she wouldn't be wearing uniform; a nurse never seemed a nurse unless she was in an apron and cap. As though her companion had read her thoughts, Mrs Pringle observed, 'I've got some white dresses for you, dear—you don't mind? There's that dressing, and just in case I should have to stay in bed...'

'How thoughtful of you, Mrs Pringle. I'll wear uniform all the time if you want me to.'

Her companion was shocked. 'Good heavens, no, dear—you're on holiday, at least, more or less—besides, I don't want any of my friends to know about me. I shall say that you're the daughter of an old friend come to spend a couple of weeks with us—will that do?'

'Very well, I should think.' Eloise looked out of the window. 'We're almost there; I'm quite excited, I've not been in a plane before.'

Mrs Pringle was looking at herself in a pocket mirror. 'I hate them,' she said, 'but they're quick. The driver will see to our luggage and if I give you the tickets do you think you could cope?'

It was all a little strange but straightforward enough; Eloise coped and presently found herself sitting beside Mrs Pringle, watching the runway under the plane slide away at an alarming speed. She wasn't sure if she liked it, so she looked away and didn't look again until they had left the ground beneath them.

It was similar to travelling in a bus, she discovered, and once over her initial uneasiness, she peered down through the gaps in the cloud and saw that they were already over the water. It seemed no time at all before her companion pointed out the Dutch coast, flat and very tidy, far below them, the sea frothing endlessly at its unending sands.

Mijnheer Pringle was waiting for them and at first sight Eloise was disappointed; she hadn't met him before, but his wife had always spoken of him with such warmth that Eloise had formed a picture of a commanding man, handsome and self-assured. And here he was, short, middle-aged and a little stout, with a round cheerful face from which the hair was receding, and not in the least good-looking. Nor was he commanding, although the porter seemed to treat him with respect. He embraced his wife carefully as though she were something precious and porcelain and then turned to Eloise, to shake her hand with a surprisingly hard grip and bid her welcome in fluent English. 'The car's here,' he said, and took his wife's arm. 'Shall we go straight home or would you like to stop somewhere for coffee?' He looked anxious. 'Should you rest for an hour or two, Debby? We could go to an hotel.'

Mrs Pringle gave him a loving look. 'I never felt better, Cor.' She glanced at Eloise. 'We had a very quiet flight, didn't we, dear? and I'd love to go home…'

Mijnheer Pringle drove well, his wife beside him and Eloise in the back of the car. He kept up a steady flow of conversation, pointing out anything which he thought might be of interest to her and making little jokes. He was as brave as his wife, and she liked him. When he asked: 'Do you not wonder why I, a Dutchman, should have so English a name?' she said, surprised: 'Well, I never thought about it—but of course it is English, isn't it? I've always said Mrs Pringle, but that's wrong, isn't it? It's Mevrouw. But you're Dutch, Mijnheer Pringle, so why…?'

'My grandfather came here when he was a young man and married a Dutchwoman, and my father was of course born here and married a Dutchwoman in his turn, so that I am truly Dutch although I have married an Englishwoman—amusing, is it not?' He added: 'And my good fortune.'

Eloise saw him glance sideways at his wife and smile; it must be marvellous to be loved like that; the kind of love which would surmount illness and worse. Perhaps somewhere in the world there was someone like Mijnheer Pringle waiting for her. It would be nice if he were tall and handsome, but that didn't matter very much; it was being loved that mattered. She thought briefly of the very few young men who had shown any interest in her, and even that had been casual. She wasn't eye-catching and she hadn't been any good at pretending to love someone when she didn't; they had found her amusing but shy and old-fashioned, and mostly treated her in a brotherly fashion, before long telling her all about some wonderful girl they had met and asking her advice. It had been a little lowering.

They stopped in Zwolle and had lunch. They were about halfway, Mijnheer Pringle told her, and would be able to travel fast on the motorway for almost the whole journey. 'Although the last few kilometres are along narrow dyke roads—real country, pasture land mostly; with plenty of big farms although the villages are small.'

'It sounds lovely,' said Eloise, and meant it, for she was a simple girl with simple tastes; she had disliked London even while admitting its charm and she had done her best to overcome that dislike because as far as she could see she would have to stay there for the rest of her working days if she wanted a good job in a good hospital. She observed suddenly, thinking her thoughts aloud, 'A lot of English nurses work over here, don't they?'

'Indeed they do.' Mijnheer Pringle was scrutinising the bill with such intensity that she had the uncomfortable feeling that he might not have enough money to pay it. 'Perhaps you like the idea, Eloise?' he asked her kindly, counting out notes with care.

'Well, it might be fun, but there's my mother—she really wants to go back to Eddlescombe, you know.'

Mevrouw Pringle gathered up her handbag and gloves. 'Well, things do happen,' she remarked vaguely. 'I'm ready whenever you are.'

It was still afternoon when they reached Groningen and Eloise looked round her eagerly, craning her neck to see everything at once and quite failing to do so; she was left with a delightful hotchpotch of tall, narrow houses, canals, bridges, a great

many cyclists and even more people hurrying to
and fro, darting into the streets and disappearing
round tantalising corners.

'You shall come whenever you wish,' Mevrouw
Pringle promised. 'I don't care for towns much—
I like to sit about at home, being lazy.' She spoke
so convincingly that Eloise almost believed her.

Mijnheer Pringle had been quite right about the
roads. They were narrow, made of brick, and wandered through the wide landscape, perched as it
were upon the numerous dykes. And the villages
were indeed small, each a neat handful of houses
encircling a church, a caf and a shop, and lying
around and beyond the villages she could see the
farms, large and solid with great barns at their
backs, their fields dotted with black and white
cows. Looking around her, she began to wonder
just where the Pringles' house might be, and had
her answer almost immediately when they passed
through a village much like the rest and then turned
between high gateposts into a short drive bisecting
the grounds of a house. It looked a little like a
farmhouse, only there was no barn built on to its
back, although there were plenty of outbuildings to
one side of it. Its front door was plain and solid
with an ornate wrought iron transom above it and
the windows were old-fashioned and sashed, two
each side of the door and five in the row above.

There were flower beds, well laid out, and shrubs and trees carefully sited; it looked peaceful and homely and exactly what Eloise had hoped for. When Mevrouw Pringle said eagerly: 'Here we are—I do hope you'll like it here, Eloise,' she replied that yes, she would, quite sincerely.

Inside was like outside; the rooms lofty and light, furnished with large comfortable chairs and solid tables and cupboards. The carpets were thick underfoot and the curtains were equally thick velvet, fringed and draped, not quite to Eloise's own taste but nonetheless very pleasing. But she had very little time to examine her surroundings; her patient was tired now and made no demur when her husband suggested that perhaps an hour's rest would be just the thing. They all went upstairs, Mijnheer Pringle explaining as they went that Juffrouw Blot, the housekeeper, would be along with a tray of tea just as soon as his wife was on her bed. 'We guessed that you would be tired, my dear, and you can have a good gossip with her later on, when you're rested.'

Alone with Mevrouw Pringle, Eloise quietly took charge, changed the dressing deftly, took off her patient's dress and tucked her under her quilt.

'Your room, Eloise,' protested Mevrouw Pringle. 'There's been no time to show you...here's

Juffrouw Blot with my tea, she can take you…and
ask Cor for anything.'

Eloise made soothing little sounds while she tidied the room, was introduced to the housekeeper,
a stoutly built middle-aged woman who smiled and
nodded and talked to her for all the world as
though she could understand every word, and then
followed her obediently across the wide landing to
the room which was to be hers.

It was a pleasant apartment, lofty like all the
other rooms in the house, and comfortably furnished with good taste if without much imagination. Eloise unpacked her bag, tidied her hair and
did her face, peeped in at Mrs Pringle to make sure
that she really was asleep and went downstairs.

Mijnheer Pringle was lying in wait for her.
'She's all right?' he asked anxiously. 'Such a long
journey, but she would insist…it is good of you to
come…' He looked away for a moment. 'Her doctor will be coming this evening—our friend too.
He will talk to you and explain…'

'Explain what, Mijnheer Pringle?' She knew the
answer already, though.

'Well—Debby has had this operation, you will
have been told about that, of course. What you
weren't told is that she is going to die very soon—
weeks, perhaps less. She doesn't know that; they
told her six months or more, got her on her feet

and allowed her home because that was what she wanted...' He sighed, one of the saddest sounds Eloise had heard for a long time. 'She's to do exactly what she wants,' he went on, 'because nothing can make any difference now. I hope that if she needs you and your holiday is finished, there will be some way of keeping you here. She has taken a fancy to you, you know—she has always been fond of your mother.' He cleared his throat. 'I'm determined that she shall be as happy as possible for these last few weeks.'

Eloise swallowed the lump in her own throat. 'Of course, and if she wants me to stay, I think it could be arranged; you would have to contact the hospital, of course—her doctor could help there. And if there's anything I can do to help, will you let me know?'

He nodded. 'Thank you. Shall we go and have tea? It's been taken into the sitting room.'

There was no milk with the tea, drunk from small cups which held only a few mouthfuls. Eloise, dying of thirst, was debating whether to ask for a third cup and run the risk of being considered greedy when Juffrouw Blot opened the door, said something to Mijnheer Pringle and flattened herself to allow a visitor to enter the room. The man who had sent her the basket of fruit; her firm little chin dropped and her eyes rounded in surprise—a surprise which he didn't appear to share, for his: 'Ah, the pineapple girl,' was casual to say the least as he crossed the room to shake Mijnheer Pringle's hand.

'You know each other?' queried that gentleman.

'No,' said his visitor cheerfully. 'That is to say, no one has introduced us, although we have met.'

Mijnheer Pringle looked puzzled, but he was a stickler for good manners. 'Eloise, this is Doctor van Zeilst, our very good friend. Timon, this is Miss Eloise Bennett who has kindly consented to spend her holidays with Deborah.'

'I know.' The doctor grinned at her. 'News travels fast in hospitals, doesn't it?'

'Apparently.' She looked at him coldly, quite put out because he had shown no pleasure at meeting her again. 'I believe I have to thank you for your gift of fruit.'

'Healthy stuff, fruit.' He nodded carelessly and turned to Mijnheer Pringle. 'How is Deborah?' and then: 'No, I'd better ask Nurse that.'

He looked across the room, smiling faintly, but for all that she sensed that she was now the nurse giving a report to the doctor. She complied with commendable conciseness, adding: 'I know little about Mevrouw Pringle's stay at the nursing home, only what she has told me herself—I've had no instructions...' Her voice held faint reproach.

He must have heard it, for he said blandly: 'Done deliberately. Sir Arthur felt that in this case, the fewer people who knew the truth, the better. However, I'll go into the whole thing with you presently.'

He smiled nicely at her and with a word of apology began to talk to Mijnheer Pringle in their own language. After a few minutes she was a little taken aback to hear him observe: 'You don't have to look like that, we're not discussing you.'

She lifted her chin. 'I didn't for one moment imagine that you were.'

'Splendid, touchy females stir up the worst in me.' He was smiling again. 'Shall we have our little talk now? It seems a good opportunity; Mijnheer Pringle has some work to do.'

When they were alone he sat down opposite her. 'You know Mevrouw Pringle well?'

'No, not really—she's my mother's friend—oh, for a very long time. She used to visit us when we lived in Eddlescombe, but I've not met Mijnheer Pringle before.' She added soberly: 'It's very sad.'

He answered her just as soberly. 'Yes, it is, but it would be a good deal sadder if Mevrouw Pringle were to linger on for months in discomfort and perhaps pain, and later spend the last inevitable weeks in hospital. I think sometimes the longing to be in one's home is worse than the pain. Her husband and I are only thankful that this won't be necessary in her case.' He crossed his long legs, contemplating his beautifully polished shoes. 'I'll outline the case for you.'

Which he did, clearly and concisely in his quite perfect English, pausing now and then to allow her to ask questions. 'So there you have it,' he concluded. 'The haemoglobin is going down fast and nothing we can give her will check it now; her spleen, her liver…' he shrugged his great shoulders. 'The opiate we're giving her is strong, you will have noticed that; don't hesitate to let me know if it doesn't give enough cover. I shall come each day and you can telephone me at any time.'

'Do you live close by?' asked Eloise, and went delicately pink because it sounded as though she were being curious.

'I can be with you in ten minutes.'

He could have told her a little more than that, surely, but he didn't, merely went on to discuss the various small nursing duties she would be called upon to undertake. 'And you will remember that no one—and that means no one, is to know about Mevrouw Pringle's condition.' It sounded like an order.

'I am not a gossip,' she assured him coolly, 'and you seem to forget that I'm a nurse.'

She was quite outraged by his easy: 'Yes, I find

I do, frequently.' But before she could frame a suitable reply to this, he went on: 'Will you be lonely here? It is very quiet—there are plenty of friends around but no bright lights and most of the young men are bespoke.'

There was no end to his rudeness. 'I can manage very well without bright lights,' she told him crossly, 'and I'm not accustomed to being surrounded by young men, so I shall hardly notice their absence, shall I?'

He laughed softly. 'I say, you have got a sharp tongue, dear girl. Might one venture to suggest that if you took the edge off it the young men might be more prone to surround you?'

She said flatly: 'Young men like pretty girls.'

'Young men, yes.'

Absurdly she flared up. 'Are you suggesting that I'm only suitable for a middle-aged widower with a string of children...?' She stopped because he was laughing at her, and anyway the conversation had got completely out of hand.

His next question surprised her. 'What did you do before you trained as a nurse?'

'I helped my father—he had a bookshop, he sold rare books and engravings.'

'Straight from books to patients—no fun, then. How old are you?'

She had answered him before she had had time

to think that it was no business of his. 'Twenty-three.'

He nodded his head thoughtfully. 'Just right,' he observed, and taking no notice of her puzzled look, went on in a practical voice: 'Now this is what we will do. Mevrouw Pringle is to do exactly what she wishes—shopping trips, visits to friends...do you drive, by the way?'

'Well, Father had a little van, and I used to drive that, but I haven't driven much since we moved to London.'

'You have your licence with you? Good; it will be best if you go everywhere with her and if you're driving she'll not suspect.'

Eloise said helplessly, not liking the idea: 'But it's years—besides, it's on the other side of the road...'

The doctor got to his feet, unfolding his enormous frame slowly, until he seemed to tower over her. 'We'll have ten minutes in my car now,' he told her. 'I'll soon see if you can cope.'

She found herself being led outside to where a dark grey Rolls-Royce convertible stood before the front door. She stopped short when she saw it. 'Is that yours?' she wanted to know urgently, 'because if it is I can't possibly drive it.'

He didn't even bother to answer her, but opened the door and stood there holding it until she got

in, then he settled himself beside her and said: 'Off
we go.'

She went; there was nothing else to do anyway,
pride forbade her from getting out again. She fum-
bled for a few minutes, not understanding the
gears, terrified of accelerating too hard and shoot-
ing through the bushes on either side of them, turning on the lights—even blowing the horn. To none
of these errors did he respond, merely sitting quietly looking ahead of him while she wobbled down
to the gate, to turn obediently when he uttered a
laconic: 'Left.' But on the road her terror gradually
subsided; true, she was driving a Rolls and if she
damaged it heaven only knew what its owner
would do to her, even though the whole thing had
been his idea. She gripped the wheel firmly; she
would show him, after all, even if the van had been
small and old, she had driven well. After a few
kilometres along the quiet road she even began to
enjoy herself.

'Very nice,' said the doctor, 'and perfectly safe.
One doesn't expect to find a girl driving with such
cool. On the rare occasions—the very rare occasions, when I have been persuaded to let a girl take
the wheel, she has invariably flung her hands into
the air and squawked like a frightened hen after
the first few yards.' His sidelong glance took in the
pinkness of her cheeks. 'Mevrouw Pringle has a

Citroën, easy to drive and quite small. You'll be all right. Now stop, and we'll go back. I've several more calls to make.'

He didn't talk as he drove back, fast, relaxed and very sure of himself, and Eloise, in a splendid muddle of vexation at his manner towards her and pride at her prowess, didn't speak either.

At the house he opened the door for her and ushered her into the hall, saying quietly: 'If I know Deborah Pringle, she will be in the sitting room...' And he was right; she was, smiling from a white face while she greeted them, assuring him that she was rested and had never felt better and was already planning some amusements for Eloise. 'And Timon,' she begged, 'don't dare suggest examining me today.'

He laughed gently and took her hand. 'It's delightful to see you again, Deborah, and I've no intention of spoiling your homecoming—besides, I've two more patients to see on my way home and then evening surgery. How about tomorrow? In the morning before you get up—ten o'clock. Nothing much, you know, just a check-up.'

He said goodbye and wandered to the door. 'I'll see myself out.' He gave Eloise a casual nod as he went.

'Such a dear man,' murmured Mevrouw Pringle. 'You'd never think he was a doctor, would you?

So relaxed—I always feel he should be sitting by a canal, fishing.'

'Perhaps he does when he's got the time,' suggested Eloise.

'He's too much in demand, and not only as a doctor. He's something of a catch, my dear, only no one's caught him yet, although there are one or two girls…' She paused, leaving Eloise to conjure up pictures of any number of raving beauties doing their best to snap up the prize. The idea made her feel a little low-spirited and she told herself it was because not being a beauty herself, she couldn't have the fun of competing with them, rather the reverse; she could see that their relationship was going to be strictly businesslike, excepting of course when he chose to find her amusing.

'I daresay he feels very flattered,' she remarked airily, and went on to suggest that her patient might like to have an early night, and how about supper in bed. She was glad she had suggested it, because Mijnheer Pringle threw her a grateful look and added his voice to hers, and she spent the next hour making Mevrouw Pringle comfortable for the night and then went downstairs again to sit and read in the drawing room while Mijnheer Pringle went to have a chat with his wife; he took a bottle of sherry and some glasses with him and Eloise applauded his action.

Presently he came downstairs again and they dined in the rather severe dining room on the other side of the hall, while her host kept the conversation to trivialities, concealing his true feelings with a flow of small talk which lasted until she felt she could excuse herself and go up to bed. She went to see Mevrouw Pringle on the way, to give her her tablets and warn her that she was to ring for her if she needed anything during the night, and an hour later, when she crept back to take another look, it was to find her patient sleeping quietly, so that she could go to her own bed with a quiet mind. It had been a long, eventful day, and surprising too. She had never expected to meet the doctor again, although she admitted to herself that she hadn't really forgotten him, only tucked him away in the back of her mind. It was a pity that he had no interest in her whatever, but then why should he? Especially if he could take his pick of all those girls her patient had hinted at.

Tired though she was, Eloise got out of bed and went to peer at herself in the dressing table mirror. It was a triple mirror and she had a good look at her face from all angles. Not even the most conceited of girls could have considered herself pretty; her nose was just a nose, her mouth far too wide, and she didn't care for hazel eyes. Her hair, long and shining and fine, she disregarded; it was all the wrong colour. 'Tint?' she asked herself. 'Something chestnutty?' and then giggled; it was doubtful if the doctor would notice even if her hair were pink. When he had looked at her it had been with the detached gaze of someone who would have preferred to be looking at something—or someone—else. She sighed, hopped back into bed, and went to sleep.

CHAPTER THREE

DOCTOR VAN ZEILST arrived punctually the next morning, and the examination he gave his patient was meticulously thorough. When he had at length finished he sat back and said easily: 'You're a wonder, Deborah.' He glanced at Eloise, standing quietly close by. 'But will you promise me to do exactly what Nurse advises? Otherwise have all the fun you like.'

Mevrouw Pringle chuckled. 'I intend to, Timon.' She hesitated. 'I suppose there's no chance that they were wrong?'

He answered her gravely. 'No, my dear, and I would be a coward if I pretended otherwise. On the other hand, no one can say exactly how long—six months has so often turned out to be a year, two—even six.'

She brightened. 'That is what Eloise said, but I hardly dared hope…'

'Well, do. What excitements are you planning?'

'A dinner party—all our friends. I want them to meet Eloise, and besides, it will be nice for Cor, he's had a rotten time lately. You'll come?'

'With pleasure—when is it to be?'

'Soon. I'll ask the van Eskes and the Haagesmas and the Potters, and there'll be us and Eloise—and you, of course. Who would you like me to invite for you?'

The doctor allowed his gaze to rest upon Eloise, who, just for a few blissful moments, found herself in a state of unexpected excitement, but only for moments; he said almost at once: 'Oh, Liske, of course.'

Mevrouw Pringle hadn't missed the look on Eloise's face, nor its instant dousing. 'Pieter will be here for Eloise,' she stated. 'Now let me see, when shall we have it?'

'Why not within the next day or so?' suggested the doctor blandly. 'Liske is going away at the beginning of next week...'

'That settles it—I'll telephone everyone today and see if they can manage Saturday. Eloise, don't look so worried, everyone will speak English—besides, you'll have Pieter.'

Eloise murmured suitably and wondered if she wanted Pieter. Now if the doctor had...but he hadn't; she gave herself a metaphorical kick for being a fool; of course he would have a girl-friend; possibly a fiancée, even a wife, and why hadn't she thought of that before? And in any case, why was she getting so worked up about it? He had shown no interest in her, and she for her part had no interest in him. She made a point of repeating this to herself very firmly, composed her ordinary features into serenity, said what was expected of her when the doctor gave his instructions to her in the hall, and bade him a coolly friendly goodbye. Let him bring a dozen Liskes—she for her part couldn't care less. She tossed her head and went back upstairs to Mevrouw Pringle.

Later, rather nervous but determined not to show it, she drove the Citroën to Groningen, parked outside Mijnheer Pringle's office and walked with her patient to the nearby shops. They were bound for the grocer that lady patronised, armed with a list of comestibles for the dinner party. Juffrouw Blot had entered enthusiastically into their plans, and between them they had put together a menu which should satisfy the guests and bring nothing but praise for their hostess. It was as they were returning from this errand that Mevrouw Pringle suggested happily that they might explore the city together during the next few days. 'And we can take short trips in the car, too,' she continued with enthusiasm. 'There's such a lot to see, though I don't think I could manage the museums—you could do those on your own, or perhaps Pieter...' She left the sentence in mid-air. 'There's Menkemaborg Castle, that's only twenty miles away and a splendid example of our architecture, and Heiligeree, where they make the bells, you know.' She glanced at Eloise: 'I'm sure Pieter will love to take you out—there are some rather nice restaurants…'

For a second time Eloise found herself battling with the feeling that Pieter would be a poor substitute for the doctor, and this time she managed to succeed. 'He sounds nice, your Pieter,' she observed, and was rewarded by her companion's happy smile. The rest of their outing was taken up with a eulogy of the young man—a paragon, by all accounts, although Eloise felt gloomily sure that when they did meet he would turn out to be a head shorter than herself and of a serious nature.

They passed the next day or two very comfortably. Mevrouw Pringle appeared to be very much the same. She slept a little, ate a little, and Eloise, ever watchful, could see no worsening in her condition, although her pallor at times was alarming enough.

Doctor van Zeilst called each day, joked gently with his patient, encouraged her to amuse herself in any way she wished and brought tickets for a concert in Groningen. 'Your favourite,' he pointed out, 'Shostakovich—in three weeks' time; I got them in good time; you know how quickly they sell out.'

Three weeks was a long way ahead. Eloise could see that her patient was thinking the same thing and getting a degree of security from it, just as the doctor had intended, she suspected.

'You'll come too?' asked Mevrouw Pringle, and Eloise pricked up her ears at his reply:

'Yes, Liske will be back. I thought we might make up a party and go back to my place afterwards.'

He spoke casually and Eloise could see that Mevrouw Pringle believed him, that she would feel well enough to do what he suggested, although it be quite beyond her strength. When he asked carelessly: 'What do you think, Nurse?' she answered cheerfully. 'It sounds delightful,' and wished heartily that he would call her anything but Nurse, in that cold, professional manner.

They went next day to see the bell factory, but Mevrouw Pringle was so weary by the time they got home that Eloise trotted out a variety of reasons why they should remain quiet the next day. 'Look,' she pointed out diplomatically, 'if you have breakfast in bed as usual and then stay in bed for an hour or so, we could get all the details for your dinner party arranged in peace and quiet; there are bound to be interruptions if you're downstairs.'

It seemed to her that her patient was only too ready to agree and although she was her usual merry self when Doctor van Zeilst paid his visit, it was obvious that she wasn't quite as well as she had been. But he made no comment, only as Eloise accompanied him to the door did he remark: 'Not so good, is it, Nurse? But only what we expected. You're doing very well, though. Try and keep her in bed for as long as possible tomorrow, and see that she rests until the last possible moment before the guests arrive. I've passed the word around that she is still convalescing, so no one will stay late.' He stopped at the doorstep and turned to look at her. 'You are quite happy here?'

'Yes, thank you, Doctor.' Her voice held its usual calm and she said no more than that, for she suspected that he was being polite and at the same time making sure that she wouldn't pack her bag and leave him to find someone else to nurse Mevrouw Pringle. He surprised her by saying: 'I'm glad. Most girls would dislike the quiet.'

'Well, I like it. I like Mevrouw Pringle too.' When he gave a careless nod she went on rather tartly: 'I did tell you that she is an old friend of my mother, and I was born and bred in the country—I much prefer it to town life.'

He nodded again, staring at her. She thought he was going to say something more, but he didn't, only smiled briefly, got into his beautiful car and drove himself away.

It took all of Eloise's ingenuity to keep Mevrouw Pringle in her bed the next morning, but by dint of getting Juffrouw Blot to come upstairs and discuss the last details for the evening, as well as her husband's soothing company, she contrived to prolong it until midday, and by mid-afternoon Mevrouw Pringle was ready enough to rest once more while Eloise laid out her dress for her, fetched up a tray of tea and finally persuaded her to take a nap.

Pieter was to arrive some time after tea. He came just as Eloise, the tray in her hands, came downstairs, and it was just as she had feared; he was indeed a head shorter than she was, nice looking enough even if inclined to faint corpulence, and already going a little thin on top. He was dressed with almost finicky neatness; he would be the sort of man who poked around the kitchen to see if his wife had cleaned the saucepans properly... She dismissed the thought as unkind and smiled at him as he crossed the hall towards her.

'You must be Eloise.' He spoke good English with a marked accent. 'What a big girl!'

Eloise ignored that. 'How do you do?' she said politely. 'You must be Pieter.' She remained on the last tread of the staircase so that he was forced to look up at her quite some way. 'Mevrouw Pringle will be delighted to see you; she's sleeping at present.'

He said importantly: 'I couldn't get home before this; I have an important job. Where's my father?'

'I believe he's in the cellar, choosing the wine.'

She watched his portly back disappear through the door leading to the basement and went on her way to the kitchen. She hadn't expected a great deal from Pieter, but even with that, she was disappointed. He had shown a marked lack of interest in his mother, and besides, he had called her a big girl. She wondered if Doctor van Zeilst thought that too. She wandered back to the sitting room, where there was a vast mirror over the carved mantelpiece and standing well back so that she could see the whole of her person, studied her reflection.

'He was right,' she observed to the empty room, and was startled into a squeak of fright when Doctor van Zeilst asked from the door behind her: 'Who was right, and what did he say?'

She was still so indignant that she didn't stop to consider her answer, but even as she uttered the words she would have given a great deal to have taken them back; there was nothing to do but wait for his laugh. But he didn't laugh. 'A girl, yes— but big? No.' He put his head on one side and studied her at his leisure so that she drew in a sharp indignant breath, a tart retort on her tongue, but before she could voice it he went on with impersonal kindness: 'Most of the women in this part of the world are tall and generously built—a good thing too, for we men would look silly if our women didn't match us for size.'

'Oh, do you mean that? But I'm not Dutch.'

He said kindly: 'No matter, you're quite all right as you are.' He became all of a sudden business-like. 'Mevrouw Pringle—has she been resting?'

'Yes, almost all day. Do you suppose she'll be able to hold out? I mean, everyone is coming at half past seven, supposing no one goes until eleven o'clock or later?'

'I've thought of that,' he told her easily. 'A phone call for me and I'll take Liske with me, of course, and offer a lift to anyone going our way—that should start the ball rolling...' He frowned in thought and Eloise asked:

'She doesn't know—or guess? You wouldn't tell her?'

His voice was silky: 'My dear young lady, you haven't much faith in my professional integrity, have you?'

'Of course I have, but surely doctors tell things to their wives.'

His brows rose. 'But I have no wife.'

'Oh,' said Eloise, breathless. 'I thought—that is, you talk about Liske...' She stopped because of the look on his face, sheer, wicked amusement.

'Fishing, Eloise?' he wanted to know softly. 'Should I be flattered?'

She felt her face grow red and said crossly: 'I'm not in the least interested in your private life, Doctor van Zeilst. And now if you will excuse me, I'll go up to Mevrouw Pringle.'

She crossed the room in her stateliest manner, her nose so high in the air that she didn't notice the small woven mat, one of many strewn about the house and the source of great annoyance to everyone in it excepting Mevrouw Pringle. It slid from under her as she tripped on it and would have fallen flat on her face if the doctor hadn't plucked her on to her feet with a powerful arm. She extricated herself from his hold even while she was enjoying it and said, very cross: 'These absolutely beastly little mats!' and bounded through the door and up the stairs. The doctor's low chuckle added to her discomfiture.

The mole velvet, when she surveyed herself in her bedroom mirror some time later, dissatisfied her; it was well cut and the material was still good, but any woman would see at a glance that it was several years out of date. She eyed its simple lines with disfavour, wishing childishly that she were small and slender and wearing clinging pastel crêpe in the very latest fashion. Her jaundiced eye failed to notice that the cut emphasised her charm-

ing shape and the sober colour complemented her
creamy skin. She tugged pettishly at its high neck-
line, fastened the gold chain which her father had
given her years ago, and went along to Mevrouw
Pringle's room, for she had dressed early so that
she would have ample time to help her patient.

Mevrouw Pringle had chosen to wear sapphire
blue silk. It matched her eyes and what was more
to the point, was easy to get into. Eloise dressed
her gently and without haste, sat her down before
her dressing table and under Mijnheer Pringle's
loving eye, did her hair and face for her and then
stood back to allow him to put on the sapphire
pendant he had brought home with him earlier in
the day.

There were a few minutes to spare when Eloise
had finished; she settled Mevrouw Pringle on a
chaise-longue with due regard to the blue silk and
slipped away with the suggestion that she should
make sure that everything was in order downstairs.
She went back presently, having admired the dinner table, eaten an olive or two and signified by
sign language that Juffrouw Blot had made a super
job of everything, to find the Pringles sitting hand
in hand. They looked happy although they had little to be happy about, but perhaps, thought Eloise,
when two people loved each other as they did, it
kept them safe from fear and loneliness and grief.

For no reason at all she thought of Doctor van Zeilst, calm, always a little amused about some small joke she was never asked to share, but surely a man who would prove a tower of strength to anyone he loved. She sighed, not knowing that she did so, and said brightly: 'There's five minutes to go—shall we go downstairs and get you settled in your chair?'

The drawing room looked pretty with the fire lighted and the lamps switched on. Mevrouw Pringle expressed pleased satisfaction at its appearance and had just settled herself when the first guests arrived; Eloise thought that she looked like a happy child at a party as she greeted them; the Potters, old friends and older than the Pringles, a little staid perhaps, but charming. They made all the proper remarks about their hostess, joked a little with their host and were kind to Eloise, as were the Haagesmas and the van Eskes when they arrived, drawing her into their friendly circle, speaking English so that she shouldn't feel shy. They had almost finished their drinks when Pieter came in with the excuse that he had had to return to Groningen. His manner implied that it had been a matter of grave urgency which had taken him there and his audience murmured sympathetically; except for Eloise, who considered him too self-important by far.

It was a pity that he caught sight of her at that

moment and started to make his way towards her just as the door opened once more; Doctor van Zeilst and his Liske, as eye-catching a girl as Eloise had feared, and contrary to the doctor's assurance, she was the exception to every rule; small and willowy, with guinea-gold hair and bright blue eyes, and as if that wasn't enough, she was wearing pastel silk cunningly draped and probably, Eloise guessed sourly, it had cost a small fortune to achieve such simplicity. The mole velvet became all at once the most hideous garment in the room and she herself exactly what Pieter had said—a big girl.

The doctor's companion shared her view—not in so many words, of course, but the blue eyes took in Eloise in one sweeping glance, and although the girl smiled and shook hands and murmured pleasantly, she was left in no doubt as to what her new acquaintance thought of her, for the delicately made up eyes were full of cold amusement and the pretty mouth wore a faint sneer.

The doctor, looming behind his pretty companion, wished her a bland good evening, his eyes on her face, and then went to speak to the other guests, taking Liske with him and leaving Eloise to entertain Pieter, who had reached her side by now and in fact, she quickly discovered, needed no entertaining at all, as he talked about himself, pausing only now and then to allow her to murmur suitably. It was quite a relief when they all went in to dinner, even though it was short-lived, for he was sitting beside her. But Mijnheer Potter was her other neighbour, and after giving Pieter her attention for the whole of the soup, she felt free to talk to the older gentleman, who entertained her with a gentle flow of small talk which was a nice relief from Pieter's self-important utterances.

The table was a circular one and over the elborate centrepiece, she could see the doctor, Mevrouw Pringle on one side of him and Liske on the other. Once or twice he caught her eye, but his glance was brief and abstracted. Only towards the end of the meal did she find him staring at her again, and this time he smiled, a slow smile which sent her heart tumbling against her ribs and left her short of breath. She took care not to look that way again until, dessert eaten, Mevrouw Pringle suggested that they should all go to the drawing room for coffee. She cast Eloise a quick glance as she spoke, and Eloise, rightly interpreting it as a plea for help, made her way round the chattering guests and unobtrusively gave her an arm with the laughing remark that she had hardly spoken to her hostess all the evening, just in case anyone had noticed, and out of earshot for a moment she whispered urgently: 'Are you in pain? Do you want a tablet?'

Mevrouw Pringle shook her head. 'No dear—
just suddenly tired, but only for a moment. It
seemed a long way to the drawing room.'

Somebody had noticed. The doctor was beside
them now. 'Tired?' he murmured. 'We'll each take
an arm—no one has noticed, don't worry, Debby.
Sit in your chair for the rest of the evening and
Eloise shall stay with you and bear the brunt of
any conversation.' He added in a cheerful, rather
loud voice: 'I love that dress, my dear—I've not
seen it before. Blue always suits you...'

He turned to include the Potters in this remark,
for they had come close enough to overhear, but
by then they had reached the drawing room and
the doctor, settling Mevrouw Pringle in her chair,
wandered off without a word or a look at Eloise.
But he had told her to stay, so stay she did, man-
aging to take Mevrouw Pringle's share of the conversation on to her own shoulders and refusing Pieter's offer to show her the conservatory, which
annoyed him very much. He was a bore, she decided, and even if he had realised how ill his
mother was, he could have shown a little more
concern for her. It amazed her that two such nice
people could have such a tiresome creature for a
son.

Mevrouw Pringle's cheeks grew paler and Eloise longed for the doctor to do something, and

quickly, and true to his word, he did. It was chiming ten o'clock when Juffrouw Blot entered the room and whispered in his ear. He went away with a muttered excuse and returned almost at once with the news that he was wanted urgently at a remote farm some miles away and would have to leave at once. He glanced at the clock as he spoke and added: 'Liske, I'm sorry, but I'll have to drop you off as we go.' His eye swept round the other guests. 'Can I give anyone a lift?'

He had been right; the Potters made a move to go too, and presently the others followed suit, making protracted farewells and offering plans for future meetings, so that it was almost eleven o'clock by the time the front door was finally closed and by then Mevrouw Pringle was looking quite alarmingly exhausted.

Eloise worked fast; her patient was tucked up in bed within minutes and Mijnheer Pringle went to sit with his wife while Eloise undressed, plaited her splendid head of hair, put on her elderly dressing gown and padded back to take his place. Mevrouw Pringle was asleep, but she decided to stay with her for the next hour or so, a decision which her husband at first contested and then agreed to, agreeing that if she were needed, Eloise would be on the spot. 'All the same,' he told her in a whisper, 'I'll not go to bed yet—there's plenty of work

I can do. I'll be in my study.' He added wistfully:
'You think it was worth while? She enjoyed herself?'

'Indeed she did—and don't worry, I think she's
exhausted, but a good night's sleep will put that
right.' She knew that she was being over-
optimistic, but her soft voice was reassuring and
kind. He gave her a grateful glance and went away,
leaving her to sit in the small easy chair drawn up
to a dim lamp. There were books on the bedside
table. Eloise turned them over idly while she
thought about the evening. It had been a success
from Mevrouw Pringle's point of view and that
was what mattered. She didn't think anyone had
noticed anything untoward and even Pieter had
bidden his parents goodbye without appearing to
notice his mother's pale face. She hoped that the
doctor would come in the morning and persuade
his patient to rest for a day or two. There had been
talk of going to the Potters' house for lunch one
day soon and the Haagesmas had suggested that
they might all make up a party and dine at Menkemaborg Castle. Mevrouw Pringle would never
manage that; a twenty-mile car drive to start with,
probably a protracted dinner and then the drive
back...

Eloise closed the book she had been holding and
sat quietly, listening to her patient's breathing,

while her thoughts dwelt on the doctor and his pretty girlfriend. The smallest sound behind her made her look round. He was there, within inches of her chair, still in his dinner jacket, immaculate and calm. He smiled as she stared and got to her feet.

'Good girl, I knew you would keep an eye on things.' He trod soundlessly to the bed and stood looking down at its occupant, possessed himself of the thin wrist while he took the pulse, laid it gently back on the coverlet and beckoned Eloise to follow him onto the landing.

'Well, she stood that well,' he said, soft-voiced. 'Try and keep her in bed until I get here in the morning, and go to bed yourself, Eloise.' His blue eyes raked her. 'You looked charming this evening and I liked that brown thing you were wearing.' He grinned suddenly. 'You look charming now, even though you're muffled to the eyebrows in flannel.' He put out a hand and gently tugged at the thick plait of hair hanging over her shoulder, then bent his head to kiss her on her astonished mouth.

'And now off with you,' he urged her, 'and don't worry, I shall stay for a little while and talk to Cor. I'll look in on Deborah before I leave and if there's anything for you I'll let you know. But I fancy she'll sleep till morning.'

'I gave her a tablet when I put her to bed.' Eloise tried to keep her voice matter-of-fact. 'I usually go along at six o'clock to make sure she's still sleeping.'

'Do that.' The hand still holding her plait dropped to his side and he stood aside to let her pass. 'Good night.'

She fastened her eyes on his waistcoat. 'Good night, Doctor van Zeilst.' Her voice sounded wooden in her ears as she slipped past him and went to her room and closed the door without looking back. She set her alarm clock for six o'clock, took off the unglamorous dressing gown and got into bed, quite certain that she would never sleep. She did, of course, within minutes.

colour, him, I think. He glanced at Eloise and smiled, and she, caught up in that he was ... handsome face was kind and he wore a shrug ... moreover she ... that he was in charge and confident.

CHAPTER FOUR

ELOISE, wakened by her alarm clock, muffled herself in her dressing gown, and yawning widely, hair hanging anyhow around her shoulders, crept along to Mevrouw Pringle's room. Doctor van Zeilst was there, standing with his back to the curtained window, doing nothing. She swallowed a yawn half way, choked on it and with a glance at her still sleeping patient, asked urgently: 'What's happened?'

'Nothing, and you don't need to look like that, pineapple girl, you're dead on time—you said six o'clock, and six o'clock it is. I was called out on a case and it seemed a good idea to call in on my way back—Cor left the side door open.'

She rubbed her eyes like a sleepy child. 'Yes, but...'

He came closer to the bed and looked down at his sleeping patient. 'We have been friends for a long time now,' he told her softly. 'The least I can do is to make sure that everything that can be done is done.' He added: 'I'm glad it's you with her.'

He bent down and took the flaccid hand on the coverlet in his own large one. 'She'll sleep for an-

other hour, I think.' He glanced at Eloise and
smiled, and she saw then how tired he was. His
handsome face was lined and he needed a shave;
moreover she noticed for the first time that he was
in slacks and a sweater.

'How long have you been out of your bed?' she
wanted to know in a careful whisper.

He left the bedside and caught her by the arm
and walked her to the door. 'Since three o'clock—
come down and make me some coffee, there's a
dear girl.'

She allowed herself to be swept downstairs with
soundless speed, but once in the kitchen with the
light on, she said: 'You're very tired, aren't you?
Haven't you been to bed at all?'

'Oh, a couple of hours. I shall do all right.'

She was putting on the kettle and searching for
the coffee grinder.

'Well, you must go straight to bed the moment
you get home—you could get an hour or two...'

He chuckled. 'I can't, you know. Surgery at half
past eight, then a round of visits after lunch, and
I've a teaching round at the hospital.'

She persisted doggedly. 'Well, you could go to
bed early.' She was assembling milk and sugar on
the kitchen table. 'Do you have an evening surgery?'

He was laughing at her. 'Yes, and I'm taking Liske out afterwards.'

Eloise had, for the moment, forgotten all about the girl; she said now rather lamely: 'Oh, yes, of course…'

'Of course what?'

She was watching the coffee percolate and didn't look up. 'Oh, just of course. It—it didn't mean anything, actually.' She fetched two mugs. 'Would you like something to eat?'

'Kind, thoughtful girl—yes, anything.'

She fetched bread and butter and a wedge of cheese and set them on the table with the coffee and watched him while he demolished almost all of them. Presently she said: 'Mevrouw Pringle wants to go to Groningen tomorrow, to buy some clothes.'

He held out his mug for more coffee. 'Let her; nothing will make any difference now and I want her to enjoy every minute…'

'She's such a nice person. Why should it happen to her, I wonder?'

'My dear girl, death comes to us all, does it not, and none of us knows when. Deborah is in her early sixties—not old, but she has had a happier life than many people I know, one mustn't lose sight of that.' He got up and wandered over to the sink. 'And don't think that because I say that that I don't mind her dying.'

He was nice, thought Eloise, watching him tidy away the remains of his meal, and strong enough to face up to things; he would be a tower of strength without appearing to make any effort at all. She went to the sink with her own mug and took a towel to dry the dishes and he said: 'I'm going home now, but I'll have another look on my way. Tell Cor that I'll telephone later.' He smiled at her. 'How old did you say you were?'

'Twenty-three—and you?' After all, what was sauce for the goose was sauce for the gander and she did want to know.

He didn't mind telling her. 'Thirty-seven. I'll be back some time today. You know where to find me if I'm needed.'

He was gone, leaving her to stand in the kitchen, the dish-cloth in her hand, staring at nothing in particular.

Mevrouw Pringle slept until almost ten o'clock and when she wakened ate quite a good breakfast and signified her intention of going shopping as she had planned. She was dressed and sitting in the drawing room when the doctor called. He stayed only a few minutes and when he spoke to Eloise it was with a cool professional detachment which quite daunted her, it was quite a relief when he went, with the excuse that he still had one more patient to see on his round.

The afternoon was a success. Mevrouw Pringle spent most of it in a small, very expensive shop, deciding which of the dresses she was shown she should buy; in the end she bought two. 'Such a splendid excuse to go somewhere exciting so that I can wear them,' she confided to Eloise as they were driving back home. 'Amsterdam, perhaps— we could make up a party and go to the theatre, spend the night there and show you something of the city...a little outing would do Cor good. The green would do nicely, wouldn't it, dear? and then we might go to Hilversum for dinner one evening. The grey chiffon would be just right with that lovely pendant Cor gave me.' She glanced at Eloise. 'That was a pretty dress you wore last night, dear. Did you bring any more with you?'

'Well, no—I didn't know that I should be going out...' She had no intention of telling her companion that that was the only party dress she owned. Mevrouw Pringle was kind enough to rush straight back to Groningen and make her a present of half a dozen dresses, so she added lightly: 'I must do some shopping for myself,' and then, quickly: 'I like the green, it really suits you.'

It was a successful red herring which lasted all the way home.

It was difficult to make Mevrouw Pringle rest; she declared gaily that she felt marvellous. 'And if I do feel tired, I can't see that it matters,' she pointed out gently, 'and I've such a lot to cram into six months—it seems a waste of time to rest.'

Eloise kept her voice matter-of-fact. 'Yes, it must seem so to you, but you're doing so well, if you take reasonable care those six months could possibly stretch to another six.'

Her patient agreed happily. 'You're quite right, dear—you're such a sensible girl and such a dear companion. If I had someone gushing sympathy over me I wouldn't be able to bear it. Cor knows that, bless him, and so does Timon. So I'll take your advice. What a pity Pieter is so busy, you could have had some young company.'

'I'm quite content, Mevrouw Pringle—it's like a holiday.' Eloise made haste to change the conversation: 'I had a letter from Mother this morning. She's having a wonderful time; Mrs Plunkett's brother is staying in the village and takes her out most days. They knew each other years ago, didn't they? She says she's getting fat.'

Mevrouw Pringle laughed. 'I'll believe that when I see her, but I'm glad she's enjoying herself. I expect you were both glad to get away from London.'

Eloise had brought the car to a halt outside the

house. 'Yes—we don't like living there, you know. It seemed the best thing to do at the time, but it wasn't. The moment I can get a Sister's job, I'm going to send Mother back to Eddlescombe—rent a cottage, or something. I'll have to live at St Goth's, but I shall be able to go home quite often.'

'You might marry, dear.'

'I'm not counting on it,' said Eloise flatly. 'I'm rather plain, you see.'

They had gone indoors and she settled her companion in a comfortable chair and declared that she would fetch tea for her. Doctor van Zeilst hadn't been yet, perhaps he would come in on his way back from seeing his afternoon patients. She found that she was looking forward to his visit. 'Although I can't think why,' she muttered as she crossed the hall on her way to the kitchen, 'he doesn't even see me.'

An observation which seemed true enough during the next day or so, for although he came each day, he exchanged only the barest civilities with her and the only occasions he sought her out were when he wished to discuss his patient's condition, and then, as usual, he was coldly professional.

Eloise told herself that it was silly to mind; after all, it wasn't as though they would be meeting each other for the rest of their lives. Sooner or later she would go back to St Goth's and that would be that.

She entered wholeheartedly into Mevrouw Pringle's plans for each day, took great care of her in an unobtrusive way, and when Pieter was home, which wasn't often, fended off his over-confident advances.

It was almost a week after the dinner party, as she and Mevrouw Pringle were returning from having lunch with her friends the Potters, that Eloise noticed her companion's extreme pallor. It made her uneasy, although her cheerful: 'How about a rest for an hour or two?' as they reached the house gave no indication of that, and she kept up a gentle chatter while she eased Mevrouw Pringle on to a sofa in the sitting room and tucked her in cosily with a rug. Her manner was calm and unhurried as she did so, and when she had finished she said with just the right amount of casualness: 'I'm going to leave you for a bit. I'll come back presently with tea; we can have it here and talk over the day. It was such a lovely lunch—the Potters are such dears.'

Her companion's tired face was lighted briefly by a smile. 'You should see Timon's house—we haven't been…'

'Unlikely,' thought Eloise, and Mevrouw Pringle went on: 'I don't know when I've enjoyed myself as much as I have done these last few days.

That's a splendid idea of the Potters, that we should all go to Utrecht.'

'It sounds smashing,' declared Eloise comfortably, holding back the urge to fly to the telephone and get the doctor. But that would never do; Mevrouw Pringle mustn't even begin to guess... She went unhurriedly from the room, but once in the hall raced silently to the study, dialled the doctor's number and waited what seemed to be endless minutes before she heard his calm voice. 'Van Zeilst.'

'Will you come at once?' she asked without preamble and forgetting to say who she was. 'We're just back from the Potters and Mevrouw Pringle doesn't look too good. I've put her on the sofa in the sitting room; she thinks she's just tired...' She added in a voice she strove to keep calm, 'Please hurry.'

'I'm on my way. Let Cor know.'

She heard the click of the receiver and dialled the second number, and when Mijnheer Pringle answered, said quietly: 'It's Eloise. Will you come home at once, Mijnheer Pringle? Your wife isn't well.'

She heard the sharp intake of his breath. 'At once,' was all he said.

Mevrouw Pringle was sleeping when she went back to the sitting room, her face pinched and milky pale. Eloise took an almost imperceptible pulse and waited.

She didn't have long in which to do so; she had left the front door open and it was only minutes before she heard the doctor's quick, firm tread.

He said nothing but went at once to bend over his patient, but presently he straightened up and asked quietly: 'When did this start?'

She told him, a precise report, just as though she were on a hospital ward. He nodded. 'She will probably regain consciousness, but only briefly, I'm afraid.' He glanced at his watch. 'Cor should be here.'

They heard the car as he spoke and Mijnheer Pringle came in a moment later, and as though she had known that he had come, his wife opened her eyes and smiled at him. He spoke in a perfectly normal voice. 'Hullo, darling, I thought I would come home early for tea.'

Mevrouw Pringle didn't answer, although she was still smiling. She didn't speak again.

The rest of the day was unreal. Eloise did what she had to do with the least possible fuss, saw that Mijnheer Pringle ate his meals, comforted the weeping Juffrouw Blot and made herself useful around the house and when asked to do so, sat down with Mijnheer Pringle in his study and ticked off names as he telephoned. He had remained very calm, but once or twice she had seen the look of utter disbelief on his face. Presently the truth would hit him hard and then, she felt sure, he would want to be on his own. It might be best if she returned to England as soon as the funeral was over—a decision substantiated by her mother when she was asked to telephone her. 'I shall come to the funeral,' her mother spoke with unwonted firmness. 'Poor Debby, I didn't know… Just a minute, dear.' Eloise heard her talking to someone with her before she went on: 'Mrs Plunkett's brother is staying here—Jack—I knew him years ago, he's offered to bring me by car. You can come back with us, darling.'

Eloise's calm forehead wrinkled with surprise. It was unlike her mother to be so decided about anything, and this Jack Plunkett must be a very good friend to offer to drive her such a distance. She was tempted to ask several questions, but there were other calls to make. She agreed hastily because there was no time to do anything else, and rang off.

Later, as she and her host sat over a hastily cooked supper, she mentioned it to him. 'Although I'll stay if you want me to, Mijnheer Pringle.'

But he refused her offer. 'I'm grateful, Eloise, you must know that, but there is little point in you staying and I think that it may be better if I'm alone for a time—besides, you have your job.'

And when Doctor van Zeilst joined them presently to drink the coffee Juffrouw Blot had brought, he agreed so readily that Eloise was conscious of a pang of annoyance. He sounded positively eager to see the last of her, his bland: 'What a good idea, nothing could be better,' left her feeling strangely forlorn, the forlornness turned to vexation when Mijnheer Pringle remarked that he needed the doctor's advice about something and the latter remarked briskly that she might like to go to bed early. 'I daresay you're tired,' he remarked, 'and there's no hurry for you to make your arrangements, is there?'

She almost heard him sigh with relief as she got up from the table. 'None at all,' she told him in a colourless voice, and wished the two of them goodnight before going to her room. She came downstairs again almost immediately. Juffrouw Blot would be in the kitchen all by herself, for the daily help went home at five o'clock; she might like a hand with the dishes. Eloise didn't much like washing up, but she was aware that she needed to do something to keep herself occupied; to lie in bed and think would do no good.

Juffrouw Blot was at the sink, washing up with grim determination and crying her eyes out. She had known Mevrouw Pringle for many years and Eloise realised with surprise that no one had told her that her mistress was suffering from an illness from which she couldn't recover, and the poor soul's grief was genuine—more so, thought Eloise, than Pieter, who had come home when he had been told the news, and gone again within the hour, with the excuse that his work wouldn't allow him to stay longer. She took a cloth and began to dry the plates, talking soothingly all the time, mostly English, of course, with a few Dutch words popped in at random and most of it quite unintelligible to her listener, but at least it gave some comfort.

Juffrouw Blot stopped crying presently and began to talk. She talked for a long time and although Eloise understood no more than one word in fifty, it did the poor woman good; she had had a lot to get off her chest, and now she was doing it. She tidied the sink, took the tea-cloths away from Eloise, went to a cupboard and returned with a bottle of port and two glasses. Eloise didn't much like port, but it seemed part and parcel of Juffrouw Blot's real efforts to overcome her grief. They sat down at the kitchen table and drank a glass each while the housekeeper continued to talk, and by the time they had finished she regained a good deal of her composure. She put the glasses in the sink and the bottle back in the cupboard and held out a hand to Eloise, saying in a watery voice: '*Dank U*, Miss,' and Eloise, feeling quite inadequate said: 'Not at all, Juffrouw Blot,' and added hopefully: 'Bed.'

The housekeeper nodded, shook hands once more and made for the back stairs, and when she had reached the top, Eloise turned off the lights and went back through the narrow passage which led to the hall. She was closing the door gently behind her when the doctor strolled out of the sitting room. She hadn't expected to see him and she could think of nothing to say; she gave him a little nod and crossed to the staircase, only to be intercepted on the way.

'I thought you had gone to bed,' he observed mildly.

She paused to look up at him. 'Probably you did, Doctor, but just because you told me to go to bed it doesn't mean that I did so. It is barely ten o'clock.'

He leaned forward suddenly and gave a rumble of laughter. 'You've been at the port,' he said.

That magnificent nose of his must be very sharp. She looked down her own unimportant little nose and said austerely: 'It really is none of your business, but I went to see if I could help Juffrouw Blot. She's very upset, it was a shock for her, you know, and she was devoted to Mevrouw Pringle.

It must have been hard for her to go on with her day's work, cooking meals and clearing them away...' Her voice faltered. 'She offered me a glass of port and I had one while she talked.'

'Did you understand what she was saying?'

'Of course not, but that didn't matter—she just wanted to talk.' She added for no reason at all: 'I don't care for port.'

He looked down at her gravely although there was a gleam in his blue eyes. 'You're a very nice girl.' He dropped his hands on her shoulders and kissed the top of her head. 'If I ask you very nicely, will you go to bed? It's been a hard day for all of us.'

She went upstairs at once with a muttered goodnight. He was being kind to her, just as he would be kind to anyone who needed kindness, but the ridiculous feeling that she would like to throw her not inconsiderable person on to his chest and bawl her eyes out would have to be firmly squashed. She was more tired than she thought and sad besides. It had, after all, been a dreadful day even though it had been inevitable and they had been prepared for it, but that didn't make it any the less sad; she cried all the while she got ready for bed and she was still sobbing quietly when from sheer weariness she fell asleep.

Her mother arrived two days later; two long-drawn-out days during which Mijnheer Pringle had gone through the motions of leading a normal life, talking pleasantly about various topics, discussing the daily news, receiving visitors with unfailing good manners. It was only occasionally that Eloise caught a glimpse of the grief he was concealing with such great efforts, and he confirmed this by telling her just before the first of his wife's friends arrived: 'You will understand, Eloise, that I shall be relieved when all this is over. I must have time to think, to adjust...I was of course prepared for Deborah's death, but even so it is difficult. I shall never be able to thank you enough for being of such great help to us both during these last weeks.'

Eloise had said quietly: 'Oh, but I did nothing, you know, but if I did help a little, then I'm glad. I hope you'll write to me in a little while and tell me how you're going on.' She had hesitated. 'You are sure that you want to stay here—just with Juffrouw Blot, I mean—with no friends?'

He had smiled at her. 'Quite happy, Eloise. Besides, I have Timon, and he's a tower of strength, and Pieter will be going to Curaçao very shortly and I think that I may accompany him—he will be working for most of the time, but I have old friends there. I can look them up.' He had added in a rather toneless voice: 'I won't pretend that he feels his mother's death as keenly as I do, but he is our son and we get on well enough.'

Her mother arrived just before lunch, driven by Mr Plunkett in his elderly, beautifully kept Rover. She was naturally subdued but glad to see Eloise again, and besides that, she was quietly happy about something. It took Eloise just half an hour to discover that the something was Mr Jack Plunkett. She had rather liked him when they had met; he was tall and thin and stooping a little and his grey hair was balding; he had blinked at her with kindly blue eyes through his spectacles when they had been introduced, and he treated her mother as though she were something precious. She and her parent were in her bedroom putting on their outdoor things to go to the funeral when Mrs Bennett said: 'I know it's not the right time to talk about being happy, darling, though Deborah would have been the first to want it... Jack Plunkett wants me to marry him, and I'm going to.' She hurried on: 'I know it's ridiculous; we've only just met after years and years, but I think we shall be very happy.'

The unconscious wistfulness in her mother's voice brought home to Eloise how unhappy her companion had been all the while they had lived in the horrid little flat in London, so that she said warmly: 'Darling, I had a feeling...I'm very happy

for you—both of you. He looks a poppet; marry
him just as quickly as you can. Where will you
live?'

'Well, there's a cottage in the village—do you
remember old Mrs Shaw's little house at the other
end of Eddlescombe? Well, she's gone to live with
her daughter and Jack's got first refusal…you
could come too, love.'

Eloise was putting on her gloves. 'What a dear
you are, Mother, but I won't, thank you. I'm almost sure to get a Sister's post within the next few
months. I'll live in and we can give up the flat and
send the furniture down to Eddlescombe. I'd be
able to come home for my weekends, though.' She
hugged her mother and added warmly: 'Mrs Pringle would have loved to know about you and Jack,'
and then: 'We'd better go down, dear.'

There were a great many people and most of
them came back to the house later. They left
slowly, leaving the place empty at last save for
Mijnheer Pringle, Eloise, her mother, Mr Plunkett
and Doctor van Zeilst. Eloise had caught glimpses
of him from time to time, although they hadn't
spoken; indeed he had made no effort to seek her
out, although, as she pointed out to herself, there
was no reason why he should. He was standing
now, talking to Mr Plunkett while her mother sat

beside Mijnheer Pringle, talking to him in her gentle way.

Eloise wandered off to the kitchen to see if she could give any help there, but the daily girl was there, sitting at the table drinking coffee with Juffrouw Blot, so she wished them goodbye, for she was leaving with her mother within the hour, and then strolled into the garden.

It was late afternoon and the days were drawing in, although the weather was still fine. She stood in its peace and quiet and the thought of London made her feel sick. She supposed that her mother would go back to Eddlescombe with her Jack as soon as they had dropped her off at the flat—she would have to set about the business of giving it up. Her thoughts, not very happy ones, wandered on. She would have to wait for the Sister's post, of course, but in the meantime she would ask if she could have a room in the Nurses' Home. The prospect, even with the chance of promotion and a good deal more money, seemed dreary enough. She leaned her elbows on the old stone wall which bordered the lawn and cupped her chin in her hands. She didn't hear the doctor crossing the grass, coming from the other side of the house, so that she jumped at his: 'There you are—why did you wander off?'

She glanced at him briefly. 'Well, Mother and

Mijnheer Pringle, and you and Mr Plunkett—besides, I had some thinking to do.'

'A pity Pieter had to go back to Groningen.' He frowned a little as he spoke and she thought that if he had been in Pieter's shoes he wouldn't have gone, pressing work or not. Come to think of it, what had happened to the doctor's own work—his afternoon surgery, his patients…?

She observed clearly: 'I liked Mevrouw Pringle, and I like her husband, but I don't like Pieter. What did you do with your patients this afternoon?'

He looked faintly surprised. 'Oh, I have a partner—two in fact, we stand in for each other from time to time. Are all your plans made?'

'Yes.'

'You will stay at St Goth's after your mother and Jack Plunkett marry?'

'Well, yes.' She sounded despondent without knowing it, and he said abruptly: 'But you don't really want to.'

She answered too quickly: 'Of course I do,' and almost choked on the lie, suddenly quite certain that it was the last thing she wanted to do. She wanted to stay in Holland and see Timon van Zeilst every day, preferably all day, for ever and ever. It was astonishing and rather absurd that she should discover, at this late hour and just as they were going to part, that she loved him. It was also quite hopeless, common sense pointed out, for had not the beautiful Liske already captured him? She said in a wooden voice: 'I should be going, I think—Mr Plunkett wants to leave before it's really dark.'

'Ah, yes—I almost forgot to mention it. The plans have been changed; you are all coming back with me for dinner and the night. Cor can't be left alone. Juffrouw Blot is going to the village with friends, and Mr Plunkett assures me that he can leave just as easily in the morning.'

Eloise said: 'Oh,' inadequately and thought how nice it would be to see Timon's home before she went; besides, she would see him for just a few more hours.

They set off presently, Mijnheer Pringle driving himself, Mrs Bennett with Mr Plunkett and Eloise, neatly plucked from the back seat at the very last moment, sitting beside the doctor in his Rolls.

He made gentle conversation during the drive, not seeming to notice her rather abstracted replies; she had a great deal on her mind, and most of it was him.

They hadn't gone back to the main road but had continued along the side road which ran past Mijnheer Pringle's house. It led to a village before long and then wound its way through fields to another, smaller village. The doctor slowed on the cobbles as they passed the first neat cottages, and when he reached the small square turned past the austere red brick church in its centre and drove down a lane on the further side. The lane wandered on into the fields again with nothing much to see save a double row of tall trees some way ahead, at right angles to the road, and when they reached them, the doctor swept the car through the massive gateposts on either side and driving faster now, entered an avenue where the trees were reinforced by shrubs and bushes so that Eloise could see very little of her surroundings. 'Where are we?' she wanted to know, peering around her.

'Home,' said her companion laconically as he drove round a sharp bend. And there before them was the house—old, magnificently ornate, with wrought iron balconies, shutters at its enormous windows and a steep tiled roof crowned by a circular dome.

'My goodness me!' exclaimed Eloise, and felt her heart drop into her shoes. The doctor, already out of reach, seemed even further away now by reason of possessing such a palatial home—although it might not be his. She brightened at the thought as she accompanied him up the shallow steps and in through the vast front door, only half hearing his formal welcome.

The entrance hall was large, square and light because of the glass dome above their heads, several floors away. The staircase, massive oak and intricately carved, ascended from the back of the hall, curving at the top to join the gallery on the floor above. There were black and white tiles under their feet, with a generous scattering of silky rugs upon them and two great wall tables, flanked by two equally massive chairs, cushioned in crimson velvet, faced each other from either wall. And coming to meet them through this magnificence was an elderly man, very spry, his white hair and whiskers framing a solemn face.

The doctor said something to him as he came to a halt before them, and the elderly face broke into a smile. 'We are delighted to welcome you to Huis Zeilst,' said the personage with tremendous dignity, addressing himself to Eloise.

'Bart,' explained the doctor, 'knows more about the family than I do myself; he's been with us man and boy and is our trusted friend as well as the world's best butler.'

Eloise stopped herself just in time from saying 'My goodness me!' again and said sedately: 'Oh, how nice,' which upon reflection sounded even sillier. She went a faint pink and stole a look at the doctor, to be instantly reassured by the blandness of his expression.

The whole party crossed the hall, Bart leading the way to throw open double doors and usher

them into a vast room, the magnificence of which
rather took Eloise's breath. Its walls were white,
picked out in gilt and lighted by crystal wall chan-
deliers. The ceiling was painted a rich mulberry
pink, a colour repeated in the brocade curtains and
the covers of the chairs and sofas arranged about
the room. The floor was polished wood, covered
for the most part by a needlework carpet in muted
pinks and faded blues, and the great hooded hearth
was flanked by glass-fronted cabinets, full, she had
no doubt, of any number of treasures. She took in
these delights within the first few moments; it was
only as she brought her gaze back to the group of
chairs arranged at one end of the room that she
saw Liske, rising gracefully to her feet and coming
forward to meet them with all the welcoming
charm of the perfect hostess.

CHAPTER FIVE

IT WAS A PITY that Eloise wasn't looking at the doctor's face, for a surprise as great as her own was on his handsome features, to be instantly concealed behind a bland smile. Before he could speak, however, Liske had reached his side and tucked a hand into his arm, and Eloise couldn't help but see the sidelong glance directed at herself as she did so; as plain to her in its meaning as a neon sign flashing 'hands off!'

'I telephoned,' explained Liske prettily, 'and I made that silly old Bart of yours tell me what was happening.' She pouted charmingly. 'If you had told me, Timon, I would have come over sooner— you never mentioned that you were having guests for the night.'

The doctor gave her a look which could have meant anything at all. 'I have an excellent housekeeper,' he pointed out suavely, 'and Bart, being neither silly nor old, is perfectly capable of carrying out my orders and wishes. You had no need to—er—put yourself out, Liske. You'll stay to dinner, of course?' He turned to his guests. 'What about a drink before dinner? and then perhaps the

ladies would like to see their rooms.' He smiled at
Mrs Bennett and ushered her to a comfortable
chair, ignoring Eloise completely.

He was a good host; despite the sombre occasion
he contrived to keep the talk trivial and interesting
enough to keep his guests talking easily among
themselves, although Eloise, for her part, had very
little to say. She was feeling annoyed that she
should feel a little overawed by her surroundings
and it annoyed her even more that Liske should be
so at ease, almost as though she were already mistress of the lovely impressive house. It was a relief
when her host got up to tug a thick silk bell rope
by the hooded fireplace, and when Bart came, re-
quested him to fetch someone to take the ladies of
the party upstairs.

Eloise mounted the staircase beside her mother,
Mevrouw Metz, the housekeeper a few steps ahead
of them, and the sight of the wide gallery at its
head, with its many corridors and little passages
leading from it, caused her mood to become even
more despondent. Even while admitting to herself
that she loved Timon van Zeilst, she had at the
same time almost, but not quite, squashed any romantic notions about her future. She was a very
ordinary girl, she considered, and he had money,
presumably, and good looks, a combination which
allowed him to pick and choose—and he had

picked Liske... All the same, until that moment she had cherished a faint hope, rapidly fading at the sight of so much wealth—and that wealth so taken for granted. He was in another world from hers.

She stopped as the housekeeper opened one of the doors in the gallery and smiled an invitation to her mother.

'Me,' said Mrs Bennett, happily ungrammatical. 'I expect you're next door, darling.'

Eloise smiled absently and allowed herself to be ushered into the neighbouring room, and Mevrouw Metz, her tall, stately figure quite at variance with her nice, placid face, sailed away with more smiles and murmurs.

Her room made Eloise sigh with delight—maplewood, the inlaid bedhead matching the dressing table with its triple mirror and the tallboy between the long windows, curtained in a flowery chintz. The floor, unlike the rooms downstairs, was close-carpeted in a thick cream-coloured pile which would show every mark—but how lovely it looked. There was an enormous fitted cupboard behind the first door she opened, the second one revealed a bathroom, which in turn opened into her mother's room.

Their overnight bags had been unpacked, so there was nothing to do but explore their surroundings before tidying themselves and going down-

stairs again. Eloise, applying lipstick, felt that anything she might do to her face would be of no use
in competition with Liske. She screwed up her
pretty hair in a severe fashion which called forth
her mother's protests, and arm-in-arm with her parent, went back to the drawing room.

Sitting up in bed some hours later, Eloise mulled
over her evening. It had been surprisingly pleasant
in a subdued way and the doctor had led the conversation quite deliberately round to Mevrouw
Pringle, talking easily and quite naturally about
her, so that very soon everyone else was doing the
same, remembering earlier days, recalling holidays
and meetings and parties, and watching Mijnheer
Pringle, she had seen that that had been exactly
what he had needed, to talk freely of his wife instead of trying to hide her away in his mind—
probably he would sleep soundly for the first time
since she had died. And Liske—she had had no
chance to centre interest upon herself, although she
had tried hard enough; in the end she had become
sulky and soon after dinner declared that she would
have to go home. The doctor had raised no objec-
tion to this, although he had gone out of the room
with her and seen her into her car; he had been so
long about it that Eloise imagined them quarrel-
ling—or perhaps he was coaxing her back into a
good humour. There was nothing in his face to

offer her a clue when he returned to the drawing room and he didn't mention Liske during the whole of the evening.

It was when the party had broken up for the evening that she had come upon Bart coming from the dining room with such a miserable expression on his face that she, alone for the moment, had stopped to speak to him.

'You speak English, don't you?' she had asked, and when he nodded: 'Then will you tell me what is the matter? You look unhappy—are you ill? Can I do anything to help?'

He had answered her with great dignity. 'No, miss—you are kind to ask.'

She forgot it was none of her business, anyway. 'But there's something wrong. You're upset—look at your hands shaking. If you could tell me it might help—I won't tell anyone else.' She hesitated. 'Shall I find Doctor van Zeilst for you? Perhaps he...'

He looked shocked. 'Oh no, miss. He must be the last person to know.'

Eloise sat higher against her pillows and hugged her knees and shivered a little, remembering how the doctor, speaking very softly behind them, had surprised them. 'And what must I not know?'

She had been clumsy and interfering, she knew

that now, for she had said quite sharply: 'Bart isn't well—or he's upset—can't you do something?'

The doctor had looked down his nose at her and remarked blandly: 'Certainly—if I may know what has upset him.'

They had both looked at Bart then, and he poor man, had muttered something in Dutch to which the doctor had replied briskly in English: 'You will tell me, Bart—we have known each other too long to have secrets.'

And Bart had cast her a reproachful and yet thankful look as he replied. 'It was only something which Juffrouw Haakema said—it is not important.'

'But it makes you shake like a leaf when you think about it, Bart. Out with it!'

Bart had broken into Dutch then and Eloise hadn't understood a word, which was perhaps just as well, for the doctor had looked angry, though not, fortunately, with Bart, for he had put a hand on the old man's shoulder and spoken to him in such a kind voice that Eloise had guessed that it was something for which Bart couldn't be blamed. She had longed to ask, but neither man seemed to remember that she was still there; after a minute or two she had gone away very quietly, upstairs after the others.

She lay down at last. Probably she wouldn't see

the doctor in the morning; they were to leave immediately after breakfast and surely he would have a surgery to take. Not to see him again was terrible, but certainly the best thing if she thought about it sensibly. Only she didn't feel sensible; she closed her eyes on threatening tears and after a while fell into a troubled sleep.

But she was to see him again. When she got down in the morning, there he was, sitting at the head of his splendid mahogany table in the dining room with no company at all but for an Old English sheepdog she hadn't seen before. She had expected everyone else to be there too and after a moment's hesitation at the half open door, began a silent retreat. But he must have had eyes at the back of his head, because he said pleasantly: 'Do come in, Eloise—the others won't be down just yet.'

He got to his feet as he spoke and turned to look at her, so that she really had no choice but to go to the table. 'Good morning—I thought you said that breakfast was at eight o'clock. I'm sorry, I couldn't have been listening...'

'But I did say that, although I told everyone else half past the hour. I wanted to speak to you alone.'

Eloise went a delicate pink. 'Oh—about yesterday evening.' She was talking so fast in order to get it over with quickly that she didn't pause for breath. 'I'm frightfully sorry; it was frightfully interfering of me, I had absolutely no right…it wasn't any of my business. You and Bart must simply hate me for it—I…'

He interrupted her as she took a much needed breath. 'My dear girl, Bart doesn't hate you—on the contrary, he considers you to be one of the nicest young ladies he has ever met. You wanted to help him just when he was utterly miserable—he will dote on you for the rest of his life.'

The pink deepened, and Eloise, hating it, stared down at the snowy tablecloth. 'Oh, well—how kind, though I didn't do anything.' She added defiantly: 'He's a dear old man.'

The doctor agreed gravely. 'Indeed he is. I would have given a great deal not have him so upset—as I told you, he is a friend as well as a trusted servant. But I've dealt with the matter and he is reassured, but it is you I have to thank—he would never have told me. Indeed, thinking about it, I am beginning to wonder if there have been other occasions…'

Eloise, still engrossed in the tablecloth, fought a strong inclination to ask what occasions and why had Bart been upset, anyway, since it was obvious that she wasn't to be told.

'Eloise,' said the doctor, and she looked up to see him smiling at her. 'You know, I'm inclined to agree with Bart,' and he pulled her close and kissed her soundly before she realised what he was going to do and then, while she was still staring up at him, he let her go and asked in a perfectly normal voice: 'Will you have tea or coffee?'

She drew a steadying breath. 'Coffee, please,' and she took the chair beside his because he was holding it for her. It would help the situation a great deal if someone else came down to breakfast, but on the other hand she wondered what he would say next if they were alone for a little longer.

He handed her her coffee. 'Bacon? Eggs? Kippers, perhaps—or a boiled egg?'

How could he talk about kippers when only a moment ago he had been kissing her as though he really enjoyed it? 'Bacon and eggs,' said Eloise; if he could eat a hearty breakfast and do a little kissing on the side, so could she.

It was vexing of him to observe as he handed her a plate: 'How nice to find a girl who eats properly and doesn't nibble at various diets.' He sat down again and helped himself to toast. 'No weight problems?' he wanted to know, kindly.

Eloise sugared her coffee. 'None.'

'I must say you're very satisfactory as you are. I don't care for skinny women.'

Eloise choked. 'Are you suggesting that I'm fat?'

'Just right, dear girl. Why did you drag your hair back so savagely yesterday evening?'

Really, he was a most difficult person to converse with! 'What can it matter to you what I do with my hair?'

His voice was silky. 'Ah, now wouldn't you like to know? Here come the rest of us.'

And after that there wasn't a chance to speak to him alone. Mr Plunkett declared himself ready to leave the moment they had finished breakfast, and Mijnheer Pringle had to go to Groningen, although he had consented to stay another night or two at his friend's house.

Eloise made her goodbyes quietly, this time receiving nothing but a handshake from her host and the careless, conventional hope that they might meet again at some time. It was Bart's dignified goodbye which warmed her. 'I thank you, miss,' he said with a sincerity which she found touching, 'and I shall remember you with pleasure always. I hope that we may meet again.'

A sentiment the doctor, beyond his casual remark, didn't echo. She had hoped, right until the last minute, that he might say something—anything—to her, but he didn't. It was only too obvious that she didn't matter at all. She summoned a cool smile as she got into the car behind her mother and Mr Plunkett, and she didn't look back.

'Such a nice man,' commented her mother as they turned out of the gateway into the road, and looked round at Eloise.

'Yes, isn't he?' She knew that she had spoken too quickly and too brightly by the look on her mother's face, and before that lady could embark on a gossip about him, Eloise added: 'We haven't had a chance to talk about you—do tell me your plans. It's so exciting—when are you going to get married?'

The subject kept them occupied for hours, with Mr Plunkett putting in a sensible word or so every now and then. They were to marry quite soon, and their home would be hers whenever she liked to visit them. The banns had been read already and they had thought in about a couple of weeks' time, provided Eloise could get a day or two off for the wedding.

'And what about you, darling?' asked Mrs Bennett.

'Well, we'll give up the flat, won't we, and I'll get a room in the Nurses' Home as I suggested. Could you come up to London for a couple of days so that we could pack up? Could Mr Plunkett bring you?'

He begged her to call him Jack and agreed to do anything within reason, adding a number of helpful suggestions, so that by the time they were in England again, driving at his sensible pace up the motorway to London, everything had been more or less settled.

The flat looked terrible after the subdued splendour of the doctor's home. The three of them went up the stairs without speaking and Mrs Bennett unlocked the door and they followed her into the narrow hall. When they were all inside, she said soberly: 'I don't know whether to laugh or cry—this, after all that...'

Mr Plunkett put an arm round her shoulders. 'Well, my dear, I'm afraid the cottage isn't all that grand.'

'It's perfect,' protested his future bride, 'and it's all I want, Jack.' She gave him a happy smile and looked at Eloise. 'And you, darling—are you sure this is what you want to do, leave here and live in?'

Eloise allowed herself a moment's reflection on what she did want; to live with Timon van Zeilst in his lovely house, and rear a family of tough little boys and small girls with blue eyes like their father... 'Quite sure, Mother.' She made her voice cheerful. 'It all fits in so well, doesn't it? I'm sure to go back on night duty and the Junior Night Sister leaves in a month—if I'm lucky enough to get the job they'll give me a very nice bedsitter, and I can come home and see you quite often—I might even afford a car.'

She smiled lovingly at her mother; it was lovely to see her looking so happy again. She had always been a pretty woman, now she positively glowed; Jack Plunkett was exactly right for her; calm and rather quiet and fond of her in a nice, speechless way—they would be very happy. Mrs Pringle, thought Eloise, would have been delighted. The thought saddened her, but she didn't allow it to show. 'I'll get the beds ready,' she declared, 'and make tea—we don't want anything to eat after that gorgeous meal we had on the way, do we? Mother, why don't you and Jack take a look round and decide what you want packed up and sent down to Eddlescombe? I've not quite finished my holiday, you know, I could get this place emptied. There's that man down the street who does small removals—he'd fix everything up and anything we don't want he'll buy, I daresay.'

The rest of the evening was spent making lists, measuring furniture to see if it would fit into the cottage, and deciding what to discard, and in the morning there was no time for anything at all, for Mr Plunkett wanted to make an early start. When they had gone, Eloise made another pot of tea and sat down in the silent kitchen to drink it. It was fortunate that there was so much to do, otherwise she might have moped.

It was something of a relief to go back to St Goth's a day or two later; the flat was no longer home with her mother gone and some of the unwanted furniture already sold. Mrs Bennett was to come up in a week's time and do the final packing and Eloise, when she was off duty, would help her. The money from the furniture already sold would be more than enough to buy her mother's wedding outfit. 'And a dress for you, too, darling,' she had insisted over the telephone. 'We'll have a lovely day shopping.'

Eloise had gone back to her packing cases, resolutely keeping her mind on the new dress, burying the persistent little niggle that there was really no point in trying to look chic. There would be no one—and by no one she meant Timon, of course—to see.

She was put straight back on night duty when she reported back. It was also intimated to her that if she wished she might apply for the Junior Night Sister's post. For the time being, she had decided not to ask to live in; there were still three weeks of their month's notice to leave the flat and it would be better, if she got the new job, to wait until she was made a Sister, so that she could move straight into the Sisters' Wing of the home. Everything, she told herself with hollow cheerfulness, was turning out splendidly; her mother happy and living in her beloved countryside again, and she herself with an assured future; it was ridiculous that she should feel like crying whenever she thought about it.

Women's Surgical was full and busy, and over and above that, it was take-in week. For the first few nights Eloise worked unceasingly with meals snatched when she could get them, and came off duty in the morning too tired to do more than cycle home to the unwelcoming flat and sleep.

But it was better when her mother arrived, excited and bubbling over with delight at seeing her again. They sat in the now sparsely furnished sitting room, discussing the future, and several times Mrs Bennett led the conversation round to Timon van Zeilst, hinting wistfully that it would have been nice if Eloise could meet him again.

Eloise managed to preserve her usual matter-of-fact front. 'Well, Mother dear, we didn't get on all that well, you know, and it isn't as though I were a raving beauty. Besides, there was that girl—Liske, he's going to marry her, I believe.'

'I disliked her,' declared Mrs Bennett with unwonted venom, 'wanting attention all the time. She didn't care a button about Deborah—all she did was make eyes at Timon.'

'I daresay he liked it,' said Eloise dryly. 'Now, love, where are we going to do our shopping?'

It was fortunate that Eloise had nights off; the packing up of the flat was almost done now and they could easily spare a day or two to go in search of something pretty for Mrs Bennett. She forgot, for the time being, about the doctor while they embarked on a lengthy discussion about clothes.

They had a splendid day; they hadn't been able to let themselves go in such a fashion for years, and Mrs Bennett, rendered quite rash after a period of pinching and scraping, fitted herself out with a pale blue outfit. 'For,' as she confided to Eloise, 'Jack likes me in blue and he's given me a mink stole and they will go splendidly together.' She bought a frivolous hat too, and gloves and shoes. But Eloise didn't find her shopping quite so easy; for one thing, she had decided prudently that whatever she bought would have to be worn during the forthcoming winter, so it would have to be a colour she wouldn't get heartily sick of within a few weeks, but she found something at last; a dark green wool coat, and although she almost never wore a hat, she bought one to please her mother— a velvet tammy which matched very well. It was pure good luck that she saw a jersey dress in a paler green. Not spectacular but very wearable, and even in her own modest opinion, the outfit suited her.

The wedding was only a week away now; she would travel down to Eddlescombe on her nights off and spend a day or two there, staying with Jack's sister until after the wedding. It would be lovely to see the village again and meet old friends, and when she got back to London she would fill in her application form and take it to the Principal Nursing Officer and ask at the same time if she could move into the Nurses' Home.

Jack hadn't been able to come up to London to fetch her mother back. Eloise put her on to the train and went back on night duty, where work drove all other thoughts out of her head.

The wedding was a quiet affair, but happy, too. Mrs Bennett looked pretty and happy and at least ten years younger than she was, and Eloise enjoyed every minute of it. She had been taken round the cottage the evening before and seen how well the furniture from the flat suited it. There was a dear little walled garden too, with a low arched door leading to a small paddock where, her mother told her proudly, they were going to keep chickens, and last of all, she had been shown the little bedroom set aside for her visits. 'And never forget that this is your home, darling,' her mother had said.

The village had been kind too, welcoming her

into the homes of people she hadn't seen for years, and all of them delighted that her mother was marrying again. Her mother was going to be happy; Eloise went back to the cold little flat, satisfied that her parent's future would be an untroubled one—not very exciting, perhaps...she sighed as she hung away the new outfit and went into the kitchen to get her supper. Tomorrow night she would be on duty again, but before that she would fill in the application form and go along to St Goth's and hand it in in the morning. Lying in bed later, she told herself that she should be perfectly content with her own future, too. It was as safe and assured as her mother's. And much, much more dull, added a small voice in the back of her head. She stayed awake a long time thinking about Timon van Zeilst, a fruitless exercise which ended in a sleepless night until she dropped into a heavy doze about five o'clock.

She was roused barely two hours later by the door bell, its strident peal bringing her half awake, her wits addled by its din and her lack of sleep. The milkman, she guessed crossly, and turned over, pulling the blankets over her head. But the awful noise was repeated, so that she was forced to get out of bed, wrap herself in her dressing gown and make her sleepy way to the door. If it was the milkman she would give him a piece of her mind!

She flung the door open in a pettish manner and was confronted by the doctor, his large person elegantly clothed in a car coat over a dark grey suit, his calm face freshly shaven, his blue eyes clear and alert.

She had no words and it was he who said: 'Hullo, Eloise,' and added blandly: 'I see I'm a little too early to be welcome.'

She stopped scowling then and opened the door wide. She had no notion of telling him that he would be welcome at any time, day or night, and all she said, rather primly, was: 'Not at all, Doctor van Zeilst. I didn't sleep awfully well, and I dozed off…do come in. I'll make some tea.'

He squeezed past her into the narrow hall and glanced around him without saying anything, and she added defensively: 'I'm moving out in a day or two—the furniture has gone down to Eddlescombe.'

He nodded casually. 'Of course. Go and put some clothes on, dear girl. I'll make some tea.'

Eloise started for the bedroom and then paused. 'How did you know that I was here, and why have you come? Have you been over here long? And…'

'What a busy little tongue! I had your address from Cor Pringle—he asked me to come and see you.'

Eloise swept her wealth of hair over her shoulders, conscious of bitter disappointment. So he hadn't wanted to come—he'd been asked to look her up; doing a good turn, nothing else. She became conscious too that he was staring down at her, smiling.

'I want you to come back with me, Eloise. Cor needs someone with him, and he likes you. Will that do to go on with?' He sighed gently. 'I've only just arrived in England.'

Her mind seized on that. 'Travelling all night? You must be tired and hungry. Would eggs and bacon do? Wait while I put on some clothes.'

'So kind,' he murmured, and took off his coat. 'I'll put the kettle on.'

She flung herself into slacks and an old sweater she had been wearing while she cleared up the flat, and didn't bother about her hair or her face, only washed the latter and tied the former back with a handy ribbon, not bothering to look. He had the tea made by the time she got back to the kitchen, with the one cup and saucer and a mug on the table and a half full bottle of milk. He poured their tea while she assembled frying pan, eggs and the last of the bacon.

'It's rather primitive,' she apologised as she laid the table with the odds and ends of crockery it hadn't been worth packing, and cut bread for toast.

'I am a primitive man,' he observed blandly, and

went on looking bland when she laughed. He added: 'How did the wedding go?'

'Perfectly. Mother looked so sweet, only she was a little sad because of Mrs Pringle.'

'We are all a little sad—Deborah was much liked.' He buttered the toast she gave him. 'Eloise, Cor Pringle is just about at the end of his tether, and that son of his hasn't helped. He's shunning everyone because he thinks they will be embarrassed if he talks about Deborah to them, and that's just what he wants to do at the moment. He talks to me, but I'm not always available, and then the other day he told me that he was sorry you had gone home because you would have understood and he could have talked to you. So I said I'd fetch you.'

'Just like that?'

'Just like that. I don't like to see a good man go to pieces. Oh, he'll get over it, but he has to blunt the first sharp edge of his sorrow and it helps to talk.'

She dished up three eggs and several slices of bacon and put them on his plate. 'Eat it while it's hot,' she advised him. 'Look, I'd like to help, but I haven't any more holidays due and I've been offered a Sister's post—I was going this morning to hand in my application form.' She added soberly: 'You see, I should have a secure future…'

The doctor buttered more toast and handed it to her. 'I see—well, there was no harm in asking.'

Eloise stared at her plate. 'Mind you, I don't give a jot about a secure future and even if I said I'd come I don't know how to set about it; you must see that I can't just walk into Miss Dean's office and tell her I'm leaving to look after someone in Holland—there's a month's notice too...'

He was staring at her hard. 'And if that could be arranged? If you were allowed to leave at a moment's notice, would you come?'

She took her eyes off her plate and met his blue gaze and heard herself say yes.

'Splendid. Is there any more toast?' And when she reached for the loaf: 'Bart wished to be remembered to you, by the way.'

'Oh, does he?' she smiled widely. 'I like him. You must be so happy to have someone like that in your lovely home.'

'You found it lovely?'

She popped two more slices under the grill. 'Oh, I did—so lovely it's hard to talk about it.'

'I'm glad. Have you a telephone?'

She shook her head. 'It's been cut off—there's a callbox at the corner of the street. Do you want any more toast?'

'No, thanks. I'll wash up while you dress and then go and telephone.'

Eloise eyed him, wondering if she would seem inquisitive if she asked who he wanted to speak to at eight o'clock in the morning. She had just decided that it was when he observed: 'Let me allay your curiosity—I'm going to telephone Sir Arthur Newman.' He swept the dishes off the table and began to wash up as though he had done it all his life, and Eloise, restraining herself from saying anything at all, went along to dress.

He was in the only chair left in the sitting room when she went into it, reading a newspaper, but he put it down at once and got to his feet. 'Ready? We've got five minutes.'

She gave him a vexed look. 'Well, really, you might have warned me! And we can't possibly get to St Goth's in that time—if that's where we're going.'

'Care to bet on it?' He hurried her down the empty flights of stairs and out of a side entrance and popped her into the Rolls, discreetly parked where it shouldn't have been. They were halfway to the hospital before she asked: 'Why have we only got five minutes?'

'Sir Arthur was going to telephone your Nursing Superintendent or whatever she's called; he suggested that we should be there at half past eight because that's the time he was making an appointment for us.'

'Us?'

He gave her a sidelong glance. 'Having disorganised your plans, the most I can do is to smooth your path.' He shot the car into the hospital forecourt and hurried her inside. Glancing at the clock as he swept her along, Eloise was glad she hadn't accepted his bet; there was half a minute to go.

'It's down this passage,' she told him.

'I know. I've been here before. We'll just have time to state our case before Sir Arthur comes.'

She looked at him round-eyed. 'You're going to an awful lot of trouble…'

He had stopped outside Miss Dean's office. 'Ah, but you're worth a lot of trouble, Eloise.' He kissed her quite gently on her half open mouth, tapped on the door and pushing her ahead of him, went in.

CHAPTER SIX

AFTERWARDS, walking soberly back to the hospital entrance with Doctor van Zeilst and Sir Arthur on either side of her, Eloise wondered just what magic had been wrought by the two gentlemen, neither of whom looked capable of such unprofessional practice—indeed, peeping at them in turn, she decided that she had never seen two better examples of learned men going about their dignified business.

'I hope, dear boy,' boomed Sir Arthur over her head, 'that you will be out of the country before our worthy Miss Dean finds the time to figure out that masterly rigmarole you offered her. I almost shed tears at this young lady's plight—forced, if I remember aright, to remain in this hospital just because its rules could not be bent.'

Doctor van Zeilst inclined his head and looked smug. 'I thought it quite a good effort myself.' His self-satisfaction decided Eloise that it was about time that she bore a part in the conversation.

'I'm not quite clear…' she began in an uncertain voice, and both her companions stopped to look at her, so that she hurried on: 'Has Miss Dean given me the sack, or am I borrowed, or what?'

'Not sacked,' observed Doctor van Zeilst in a shocked voice. 'You have resigned for urgent personal reasons, with the option of applying for the Night Sister's post which you seem so anxious to have, when you return—provided it isn't filled in the meantime.'

She almost wrung her hands. 'But of course it will be by then—I'll be a staff nurse for ever! Oh, I wish I'd never...'

'Tut, tut, you weren't listening. Cor Pringle is going to Curaçao in two weeks' time—I surely mentioned that? There will be plenty of time to apply for the job if you're still bent on carving a career for yourself.'

They began to walk on again, and Eloise perforce with them. At the entrance Sir Arthur bade them goodbye and bon voyage and murmuring that he was already late for his ward round, went on his dignified way. When he was out of sight, Eloise, her temper frayed by uncertainty and the nasty feeling that she had been rushed into something she didn't know about, snapped: 'Well, what do I do next? You tell me.'

'Coffee, I think, don't you?' Doctor van Zeilst smiled at her with great charm, and although her heart beat so fast at the sight of it that she almost choked, she said firmly: 'That won't help in the least.'

'Oh, it will. We need a little time while I tell you what we're going to do.'

'We? Do what? Look, you must explain…' Her voice was shrill with the beginnings of temper. 'You rush me along to see Miss Dean and cook up a story I'm sure she doesn't in the least believe—and however did you get her to allow me to resign and then apply…'

'Charm.' His voice was all silk. 'And I must add, a good deal of spade work on the part of Sir Arthur. It's amazing,' he reflected gravely, 'what one can achieve when one really puts one's mind to it.' He suddenly became businesslike, almost urgent. 'Eloise, Cor Pringle really does need someone. Oh, he's got Juffrouw Blot, but although she's a splendid housekeeper, he can't talk to her. I had to think of some way of getting you back without falling foul of hospital rules.

'I imagine Miss Dean is fully aware that they are being bent, but why not when it's in a good cause? If you were ill for two weeks, someone would take your place, would they not? I know you're worried about resigning, but she promised that you might apply for that job, didn't she? Will you stop worrying and listen to me?'

'I've been listening.'

They had been walking down the narrow, shabby street behind the sprawling hospital. Now he stopped outside a neat little caf half way down it, much patronised by the hospital staff. There weren't many people inside and they sat down at a table in the window, and after a minute or two the proprietor ambled over, gave the table an extra rub up with his cloth, took the doctor's order for coffee, and went away again. It wasn't until it arrived, hot and strong, that the doctor broke the silence between them. 'We'll go first to Eddlescombe, on our way home...'

Eloise put down her cup. 'But it's miles out of our way!'

'Let us not exaggerate; it is a couple of hours' driving from here, perhaps a little more.' He looked at his watch. 'We could be there by mid-afternoon, stay the night if your mother would be so kind as to invite us, and journey on the following morning.'

Eloise's wide mouth curved with delight. 'How super! Could we really?'

He took a lump of sugar from the bowl and crunched it up. 'We could and we will—after all, you deserve some small reward. And now if you have finished your coffee, shall we go round to your flat? You can pack and do whatever is necessary—would an hour be long enough?'

It was obvious to her that she wasn't going to be given more than that. She nodded. 'Yes, provided you do some telephoning for me—the gas and electricity—oh, and the landlord.'

The doctor lifted a finger for the bill. 'My practical Eloise! Let us get started by all means.' He swept her out into the street again and walked her back the way they had come to where the car was parked in the hospital forecourt. A few minutes later they were at the flat.

And later still, with London's outskirts already behind them, Eloise found herself driving down the M3, with the doctor, peacefully asleep, beside her. It seemed a good opportunity to explore her thoughts; there was very little traffic and the Rolls purred effortlessly ahead. She didn't know if she were coming or going, all she was sure of was that her companion knew, and that because she loved him and trusted him she was quite content to leave her immediate future in a muddle in order to please him. Common sense told her that she was being a fool; later on she would come to her senses and probably bitterly regret allowing him to rearrange her life for her.

She sighed, remembered the instructions he had given her when she had taken over the driving, and slowed the car's pace as they approached Wimborne Minster. She had driven rather less than a hundred miles at a steady, fast speed, mostly on the motorway, but she didn't feel tired as she drove carefully through the little town and stopped in its square outside the King's Head. It was time to wake her companion, but when she turned to him it was to find him awake, his eyes fastened on her. 'Nice driving,' he murmured. 'You handle her very well.'

She thanked him primly and asked if he had slept.

'Soundly, thanks to you. Shall we have lunch—it's getting a little late, but I daresay they'll serve us.'

They ate roast beef and Yorkshire pudding and followed it with treacle tart, washed down with claret. They were drinking their coffee when the doctor remarked: 'I'll drive the rest of the way—it's not far now, is it? Just over twenty miles to Dorchester and take the Milton Abbas road—you'll have to direct me. Who taught you to drive?'

'My father.'

'He did it well, though I think you're a naturally good driver.'

Eloise said thank you once more and then allowed her tongue to run away with her. 'Do you let Liske drive your car?' she wanted to know.

His eyes became very blue and cold. 'No, I do not—why do you ask?'

Perhaps it was the claret, but she felt reckless. 'Well, I thought she might...'

'And what makes you think that?' His voice was silky.

'Well, she...she was at your house when we went there, and from what she said, I thought...she seemed very at home...' Her voice petered out under his cold stare.

'Well?' he repeated, still silky, and she could see that she wasn't to be allowed to leave the matter there.

'As though she...as though you both...' She tried again. 'I thought perhaps she was going to marry you,' she finished gamely, her voice small.

He smiled in what she considered to be a very nasty manner. 'You may think what you wish,' he told her blandly. 'Shall we go?'

Excepting for giving directions when it was necessary, Eloise preserved silence for the remainder of their journey, spending her time trying out numerous apologies to herself, none of which were really satisfactory. And as for her companion, he was silent too, although from time to time he whistled softly to himself, for all the world as though he were in the best of humours—which he quite obviously wasn't.

But when they arrived, no vestige of ill-humour was allowed to show. He got out of the car, came round to open her door and then waited while she went up the path to the cottage's front door, where she thumped the knocker, tried the handle, and when she found it open, called, 'Mother, it's us!' unaware of the doctor's reluctant smile at her words.

She was answered by the opening of a window above her head and the appearance of her mother's neat head thrust out. 'Darling, what a lovely surprise—and Doctor van Zeilst, too! Come on in, I'm on my way down.'

They had barely got inside when she joined them, running down the staircase with the lightness of a girl, to fling her arms round her daughter's neck and hug her before shaking hands with the doctor.

'Oh, isn't this just lovely!' she exclaimed. 'Jack will be pleased—he's in the garden making chicken houses. Have you come to stay? I do hope so.'

'We're on our way to Holland,' said Eloise quickly. 'We wondered if we could spend the night.'

'As many as you like, you're both very welcome.' Her mother smiled at her second guest and asked guilelessly: 'Why are you going to Holland? Or rather, why did you come to England—or mustn't I ask?' She tucked a hand into his arm.

'Come into the sitting room and sit down and tell me before I fetch Jack.' She opened a door and ushered them into the comfortable little room, bright with firelight, and said: 'Let me have your coats—now do tell…'

'There's nothing much to tell, Mrs Bennett.' It was the doctor who answered her, for Eloise seemed to have lost her tongue for the moment. 'Cor Pringle isn't too well—depressed, not eating, lonely. He told me that he wished Eloise had still been with him because she understood how he felt and he felt he could talk to her—she has very kindly agreed to go and stay with him until he goes to Curaçao in two weeks' time.'

If Mrs Bennett felt disappointment at this explanation, she concealed it admirably, only darting a look at her daughter's composed features and smiling faintly. 'How did you get away from St Goth's?' she wanted to know.

'Doctor van Zeilst and Sir Arthur Newman talked to Miss Dean,' Eloise told her flatly. 'I've resigned, but I'm allowed to apply for that job I told you about when I get back—if it's still going,' she added snappily.

Her mother ignored the snappiness. 'How sensible,' she declared. 'I'm sure Cor will be glad of your company—I thought it was a mistake staying on in that house by himself. Now he can talk as much as he wants to about Deborah. You can't just turn your back on years of happiness with someone without talking about it—the trouble is, other people tend to shy away from just that because they think it makes you miserable—such a mistake.' She looked at the doctor. 'Not you, of course, Timon—you don't mind if I call you that?—I thought you coped beautifully.' She got to her feet. 'I'm going to fetch Jack, then we'll have tea. Did you get any lunch?'

Eloise answered this time. 'Yes, thanks, dear—in Wimborne. But we'd love tea—I'll give you a hand.'

She sent her mother such a beseeching look that that lady said instantly: 'Oh, yes, do, dear,' and the doctor, sitting in his chair watching them, allowed his eyelids to droop over the amused gleam in his eyes.

Jack having duly welcomed them and taken a chair opposite the doctor, the two ladies went off to the kitchen, a surprisingly roomy place, a trifle old-fashioned, but as Mrs Bennett declared, just how she liked it. They set about getting tea; scones and butter and jam and a large fruit cake as well as muffins. It was while Eloise was putting cups and saucers on a tray that her mother asked: 'Did you two quarrel all the way here, darling?'

Eloise choked. 'Mother! Not until we got to

Wimborne. I drove most of the way and he slept—
he's been up all night.'

'That accounts for that bland expression; I've
noticed it before—lack of sleep,' she went on
vaguely, 'or perhaps it was something else?' She
turned to look at her daughter, who was slicing
cake savagely.

'I expect he was thinking about Liske,' muttered
Eloise bitterly.

'That's what you quarrelled about?'

'Mother, you can't quarrel with him—he won't.
He just—just silences you. Shall I take in the tray?'

Tea was quite enjoyable. The doctor, tired or
not, was the perfect guest and Jack was a good
host, and if Eloise and the doctor took care not to
address each other directly unless it was absolutely
necessary, their companions appeared not to notice. They sat around the fire after tea, until it was
time to get supper; a sizzling macaroni cheese with
a sustaining soup first and beer for the men, and
then once more round the fire while they drank
their coffee. They didn't stay up late, although it
was very pleasant sitting there talking about nothing much, but as Mrs Bennett pointed out, they
kept country hours and besides, Timon would be
tired. She wished him goodnight, told her husband
not to keep their guest up late, and whisked Eloise
upstairs with her.

'It seemed a good idea,' she told her as they gained the small landing. 'Only one bathroom, you see, though there's plenty of hot water—you'll have time to get a bath.' She kissed Eloise gently. 'Dear child, things take so long to happen sometimes.' With which obscure remark she took herself off to her own room.

It was raining when Eloise woke in the morning, and not quite light. She got up and crept downstairs and made tea, then took a tray up to her mother's room before going back to the warm kitchen to sit in her dressing gown by the Aga to drink her own. She had decided against taking the doctor a cup. He could come down for it; if she took it, he might think that she was trying to get into his good graces. 'Monster!' she muttered crossly, filled her cup for the second time and curled up in the elderly basket chair; she would sit there in peace and quiet for ten minutes.

A plan instantly shattered. The back door opened and the doctor came in, very wet. He looked at her without surprise, wished her good morning, remarked that he had taken the car to the village garage to get filled up and asked, very politely, if he might have a cup of tea.

Eloise uncurled herself, conscious that she looked pretty awful; the dressing gown she had borrowed from her mother was too small, too short and faded, and her hair was a wild tangle down her back. She wished him good morning a little belatedly and went to fetch a mug. 'You're very wet,' was all she could find to say.

'It's raining,' he commented mildly, and took off his car coat and opened the door again to shake it before draping it over a chair.

She passed him the sugar. 'I hope you slept well?'

'Excellently, thank you.' He looked at her searchingly as he spoke, almost as though by studying her tired face he could see that she had stayed awake far too long, thinking about him. 'Shall you be ready to leave after breakfast?'

She nodded and got up once more. 'Yes. We're having it at eight o'clock—we can be away by half past. I'll go and dress. There's plenty more tea in the pot if you'd like to help yourself.'

He only smiled in reply and went to open the kitchen door for her, which was absurd of him, but nice all the same considering what a fright she looked.

It rained all day, with leaden skies and a nasty gusty wind which Eloise hoped would stop blowing before they got to Dover. Her companion was at his most amiable, although there was little warmth in his manner. She decided that he had made up his mind to be polite at all costs, maintaining a desultory conversation about this and that and being careful not to introduce any personal element. She replied suitably, and from time to time, feeling that it was her turn to bear the burden of polite talk, made observations about the weather, their journey, the countryside and the charms of Eddlescombe. Only as they sat down to lunch at the Wife of Bath in a small village just outside Ashford did she come to a halt. She sat studying the menu without really seeing it and presently, aware that his eyes were on her, said, quite against her inclination: 'I'm sorry if I annoyed you yesterday.'

She looked at him as she spoke and saw his brows lift slightly. 'Annoy me—you make me very angry, you frequently do.'

Any desire she might have had to apologise melted away into thin air. 'Well, you had no reason to be,' she told him roundly. 'I hadn't meant to pry, I only—well…' She stopped, rather at a loss for words, and he supplied them for her in a silky voice: 'Put out a feeler?' he suggested. 'Tried a little guessing? That will get you nowhere with me, Eloise.'

Nothing would get her anywhere with him. She ignored the snub and said haughtily: 'I think that I have made it quite clear to you already that I have no interest in your affairs.'

'No? I'm disappointed.' He smiled and his whole face changed. 'Shall we bury the hatchet for the moment? One day—not too far off, I hope, I shall do my best to interest you in what you so airily describe as my affairs. And now what shall we eat?'

She sighed. He was holding out an olive branch, but only as a gesture, and probably more for his own satisfaction than any intent to please her. She ate the delicious food he had ordered, and plunged once more into polite nothings by way of conversation, thinking how very foolish it was to love someone who barely tolerated you, and that with a remote civility which set her splendid teeth on edge—a reflection which bore her up for the remainder of their journey.

But she forgot her own grievances when they arrived at Mijnheer Pringle's house and she saw the pleasure on his face. He seemed to have aged a good deal in the short time since she had seen him, but his welcome was sincere, so that she knew then that she had done the right thing in coming. And an equally delighted Juffrouw Blot took her case up to her room before taking her downstairs again to join the men for a drink.

And later, when she had gone upstairs and unpacked and changed her dress, she found that the doctor was staying to dinner. She sat between the two men, one at each end of the table, and ate whatever was put before her, taking part in the talk when she was directly addressed while she wondered if and when she would see Timon again.

Not soon, she surmised, for she heard him tell his host that he couldn't stay for coffee because he had an appointment later that evening. Liske would be waiting for him, she supposed, and she wished him an austere goodnight in consequence, coupled with even more austere thanks for bringing her to Holland, although, now she came to think about it, she had no reason to do so; he had been the one who had insisted on her coming in the first place. It was mortifying to hear him say, just as though he had read her thoughts: 'You really have no reason to thank me, Eloise. It was I who persuaded you to come in the first place, and that for my own good reasons.'

She had nothing to say to that and he left very shortly after, leaving her to sit with Mijnheer Pringle and drink more coffee while he talked about his Deborah. They sat up quite late although she was tired enough to have gone to bed hours earlier, but she had her reward when he told her: 'I shall sleep tonight, Eloise; I can talk to you about Debby—there is so much I want to remember and say, and Pieter won't allow that. He says it's morbid; he thinks that I should shut her away and think of other things, but that I cannot do, and I think that you understand that. If you will bear with me for a week or two...'

'There's no question of bearing with you, Mijnheer Pringle.' Eloise's voice was gentle. 'I like to talk about Mevrouw Pringle too as well as listen to you—besides, why should you shut her away? She will always be in your head, won't she—you can't shut her out. And I think I know how lonely you are.'

'You will make some man a good wife one day, my dear. I have been depressed and perhaps too sorry for myself—Timon knows that, but now that you are here by some small miracle, I promise you I will take up the threads of my life again.'

Eloise got to her feet. 'Well, your wife would want you to, you know. She was a happy person and she would want you to be happy too. Will you remember to take your sleeping pills or shall I get them for you?'

'I will remember.' He was on his feet too. 'And I have kept you from your bed, for which I am very sorry. Tomorrow I will start afresh.'

'The garden,' suggested Eloise. 'You must keep it looking just as it always did—we could clear the leaves and light a bonfire.'

He smiled: 'That I shall enjoy—after breakfast?'

'After breakfast.'

She was even more tired than she had thought; she had intended to work out some plan for seeing Timon again, but she went instantly to sleep.

She and Mijnheer Pringle were busily engaged in building the bonfire when the doctor drove up. Eloise, sweeping leaves across the lawn at the side of the house, saw him coming up the drive and pretended not to have done so. She was muffled in one of Mijnheer Pringle's old raincoats, with a scarf over her head because the day was damp and chilly, and for a moment the absurd idea crossed her mind that he might not recognise her, an idea instantly dispelled by his loud: 'I like the outfit— are you intending to crown the bonfire?'

She shot him a cross look and said peevishly: 'Certainly not. I don't happen to be a girl who fusses over her appearance, that's all.'

'Meaning that Liske does?' he wanted to know blandly.

'Meaning no such thing,' she declared, and uttered the lie with conviction. 'And why bring her up?'

He smiled his nasty smile. 'I like to annoy you, my dear.'

He turned away and walked to where Mijnheer Pringle was happily forking the leaves and debris into a pile and the two men stood talking for a few minutes before Timon when back to his car, with nothing but a nonchalant wave as he passed her. 'Good riddance to bad rubbish,' muttered Eloise, and poked at her pile of leaves with such venom that they scattered all over the lawn again.

They were having their lunch when her host remarked: 'Timon asked us for dinner this evening and of course I accepted.' He didn't wait for her to reply, but went on: 'Shall we finish the garden this afternoon, or are you tired? We have made splendid progress.'

'Let's finish it,' suggested Eloise, her mind busy on what she should wear that evening—she hadn't anything, she concluded, and abandoned the idea of competing with Liske, who would certainly be there too. Aloud, she said: 'Have you been to see any of your friends? When the garden's finished would it be a good idea to call on them all—you won't see them for a bit if you're going to Curaçao.'

He liked the idea. 'Of course, that is a good idea—we will do that, but we must remember that Pieter is coming for the weekend.' He added with pathetic cheerfulness: 'We shall be quite gay.'

Eloise tried to imagine being gay with Pieter and her mind boggled. 'How nice—I expect he's looking forward to his trip.' She gave her companion another cup of coffee and deliberately led the conversation back to his wife.

Later, going through her scanty wardrobe in a rather hopeless way, Eloise decided to wear a grey jersey dress; indeed, with the exception of the dress she had bought for her mother's wedding, there was no other there; a variety of slacks and woollies and a skirt or two, but none of those would do. It would have to be the grey. She put it on without much enthusiasm, piled her hair into a shining top-knot, did her face with care, and went downstairs to find Mijnheer Pringle. So far the day had been successful; they had been busy in the garden until dusk, and he looked better for it, although now he looked a little tired; perhaps it would be a better idea if they went visiting the next day and gave the garden a rest—she put the idea to her companion as they drove to the doctor's house.

There were welcoming lights shining from the ground floor windows as they arrived. Eloise, getting out of the car, wondered just how much it would cost to maintain such a magnificent home; a small fortune, probably. The doctor must be a rich man—another good reason why she must forget him as quickly as possible. She sighed and then smiled widely at Bart's welcome, pleasure at seeing her again lighting up his elderly face. He took their coats and led them across the hall to the drawing room where Timon was waiting for them. He was standing at the other end of the big room, staring out into the dark grounds from the french windows, but he turned round when he heard Bart's voice, and Eloise had the impression that he had been so deep in thought that he hadn't heard their arrival, although his face was impassive and he seemed his usual unruffled self as he poured their drinks, wanting to know how they had spent their day and what their plans were for the days ahead. Eloise sipped her sherry, hating the grey dress and making polite answers to her companions' remarks. She wasn't surprised when Timon said casually: 'Liske should have been here long ago—probably she has been delayed.'

Doing what? Eloise asked herself silently, and answered her own question. Making up her mind which of her many dresses to wear. She peeped at the doctor and came to the conclusion that he was either angry or worried about something; the blandness was so very pronounced. But there was little change in his expression when Liske at last joined them, and Eloise, studying his face closely, could see no sign of the delight a man in love would surely show the object of his affections. True, he crossed the room to greet her and when she threw her arms around him and kissed him, he didn't appear to mind.

Eloise looked away quickly before Liske could see her watching them and chatted airily to Mijn-

heer Pringle until Liske came over to say hullo
with what she considered to be a smug smile, but
then she would have felt smug herself if she could
look gorgeous in a silver lamé suit, with blonde
hair bouncing on her shoulders, delicate wrists
loaded with gold bracelets which tinkled and
clashed each time she moved her useless, pretty
little hands. She was all charm and friendliness towards Eloise, who feeling that at the moment she
possessed neither of these attributes, was aware of
being at a disadvantage. Indeed, she suspected that
the horrid girl had deliberately engaged her in talk
so that their companions could have ample opportunity to appreciate the vast difference between
them. Certainly Eloise's tall, well built person
served to emphasise the grace and daintiness of
Liske.

Bart announced dinner almost at once, but Liske
lifted a shoulder and said in a little-girl voice: 'But,
Timon, I've only just got here—I couldn't possibly
swallow my drink so quickly.'

He smiled across the room at her. 'You're very
late,' he pointed out, 'I'm afraid you'll have to
leave the rest of your drink. Shall we go in?'

Liske pouted, tossed off the contents of her glass
and went to join him while Eloise got up more
slowly, conscious of her size and the inadequacy
of the grey jersey. It surprised her when the doctor

came towards her, saying casually: 'Cor, look after Liske, will you?' and took her arm.

'I can see that Cor is feeling better already,' he said quietly. 'Thank you, Eloise, you are just what he needed, you know.' He began to walk unhurriedly to the door, his hand still on her arm. 'Have you any plans for the next few days?'

'I wondered if we were to call on some of his friends? There's a lot to do in the garden, but I think he's tired, and if we gardened every day he'd get quite exhausted.'

He nodded agreement. They were in the hall now, with Bart watching them from the dining room door. 'Sunday,' mused the doctor, 'supposing we go over to my sister's place. I don't think you've met her; she was at the funeral, but there were so many there. I'll come for you and Cor about ten o'clock—we'll go for lunch.'

She felt a pleasant warmth underneath the despised jersey; he was only being kind and thoughtful, of course, but a day in his company would be something to treasure.

Dinner was delicious; thin soup, roast duckling with cherry sauce and a creamy pudding of great richness. Eloise ate with healthy appetite, enjoying every morsel, while she pondered the fact that food, served on exquisite china and eaten with solid silver, tasted so much better. They drank claret with the duckling and a delicate white wine with the sweet, and Liske, who had behaved very prettily until the mouthwatering dish was presented to her, remarked rather pointedly that she didn't dare touch a morsel of it. 'For I should hate to get fat,' she trilled, and glanced across the table at Eloise, about to lift the first morsel to her lips. You couldn't answer rudeness like that, she decided furiously, and defiantly had a second helping.

They had coffee in the drawing room and Timon talked about Deborah Pringle in such a natural, unselfconscious way that presently Cor Pringle joined in, relaxing more and more as the evening wore on, but Liske, not in the least interested, wandered about the lovely room, picking up the trifles of china and silver lying on the little tables, doing her best to change the conversation, until she declared that she had a headache and would go home.

The doctor rose, sympathised with the headache and went with her into the hall, leaving the drawing room door half open, and although Liske was speaking Dutch, Eloise had no difficulty in guessing that she was furiously angry about something. The doctor's voice, on the other hand, sounded calmer than ever. He came back presently, looking quite inscrutable, and rang for more coffee, declaring that it was far too early to break up such a pleasant evening, so that it was an hour before

Mijnheer Pringle suggested they should really go home otherwise Eloise would be asleep on her feet. So she got to her feet too, though reluctantly. She had enjoyed sitting there, listening to the two men talking quietly, joining in herself from time to time and loving the peace and quiet of the room. It was while Timon was helping her into her coat that he said softly: 'You look exactly right sitting in my drawing room, Eloise, in that pretty grey gown— you're a very restful person.' He lifted her hand and kissed it and she could only goggle at him. 'No bracelets,' he murmured, 'to drive a man insane.'

She managed to find her tongue at last. 'Oh— well, I haven't any, you know.'

He smiled down at her. 'Thanks for coming this evening,' and then in a brisker tone: 'Remember to be ready on Sunday. I shall look forward to it.'

So would she, but why, she pondered on their way back, should he look forward to it? Because he had quarrelled with Liske and wanted to teach the tiresome girl a lesson? Or perhaps she was coming too—she hadn't thought of that. It worried her all the way home and long after she was in bed and should have been asleep.

CHAPTER SEVEN

ELOIS AND Mijnheer Pringle spent the next two days visiting, first the Potters, where they stayed for lunch, then on to the van Eskes, where they remained for tea and drinks before they went back home, and on the second day to the Haagesmas, who insisted on them remaining for both lunch and dinner. And all of them, Eloise was delighted to find, talked their fill of Deborah Pringle; perhaps the doctor had primed them, she wasn't sure, but of one thing she was certain, that Mijnheer Pringle was a happier man than he had been when she had arrived. They spent the next day in the garden, in windy rainy weather, and played chess in the evening, at which game Eloise showed herself to be possessed of some skill, for her father had taught her as a child.

And the next day was Sunday. Without going too deeply into her reason for doing so, Eloise put on the grey jersey again, wrapped herself in her new winter coat and went downstairs to join Mijnheer Pringle. She barely had the time to brush him down and find his hat before the Rolls purred to a standstill at the front door and they were joined by Timon.

Liske wasn't with him; that was the first thing Eloise saw as they went outside. She was ushered into the back of the car, sharing it with Bluff the dog, who made much of her and then, at a quiet word from his master, retired to his corner. She sat, a hand on his woolly neck, as the doctor, with Mijnheer Pringle beside him, drove out of the gates and took the road to Groningen. 'It's not a long drive,' he told her over his shoulder, 'north of the city but well out in the country.'

Which meant very little to her without a map, but she was content to watch the countryside, bare with the beginnings of winter, while the two men talked quietly together. The villages all looked rather alike, small and compact, clinging to their churches in the centre, but away from them the great farmsteads squatted in wide meadows, their enormous barns, their pristine paintwork and well ordered gardens bearing witness to their prosperity. There were horses in the fields too, great powerful beasts, standing about in Sunday idleness, but the cows were indoors, kept warm against the chilly wind.

The road wound through the fields, occasionally plunging into a small copse, and it was in the middle of one of these that the doctor turned the car

into a rough lane at right angles to the road. It was
lined with trees, bare now, but the thickets on either side were dense enough. A little further on,
when they reached an open gate, the track changed
to a well kept brick surface which in its turn curved
into a sweep before a roomy house with a great
many windows, each crowned with eaves and em-
bellished with small balconies. The front door was
wide and lofty and reached by a short flight of
steps, and there was a verandah running round the
house on either side. It looked a pleasant, homely
place and as Eloise got out she could hear dogs
barking and children's voices. They all came tumbling out to meet them; a small boy, two little girls
and a young woman with a baby under one arm,
and behind her, the master of the house with a
couple of golden labradors. For a few minutes they
stood in a group while she was introduced; the
dogs gavotting round them and the children tug-
ging at their uncle's hands and then Eloise was
whisked away to take off her coat by her hostess,
a pretty girl, a good deal younger than her brother,
who begged her to call her Juliana and hoped with
the same breath that she liked children: 'For we
have four, as you can see, and we like to have them
with us as much as possible—Bram is away all
day—he's an anaesthetist at Groningen hospital,
and says he never sees enough of them.' She

paused for breath and then went on before Eloise could speak: 'Yes, I can see exactly what Timon meant when he told me about you.'

Eloise paused in the tidying of her hair. For the life of her she couldn't stop herself asking: 'Oh? What did he say?'

'That you weren't pretty but that you had beauty.'

Eloise turned to stare at her hostess, her mouth open. 'He said that? Well, he must have been joking.'

'I think not, I believe he might be vexed if he knew that I had told you. Shall we go down?'

The rest of the morning was an unqualified success; they drank their coffee in a comfortable sitting room with the children, mouselike, eating biscuits, and later they had lunch, a leisurely meal taken in a room overlooking a beautiful garden. And after lunch, lulled by the wine she had drunk and the gentle stream of conversation around her, Eloise sat with her hostess, the two little girls on either side, answering her questions. It wasn't until much later on that she realised that she had told Juliana almost all of her life's history.

But presently she found herself alone with the doctor while the others went to the greenhouses to inspect some plant or other. Juliana had dumped the baby in his lap, where it lay with its legs kicking the air, held fast by one large gentle hand. The two little girls and their brother were on the floor beside Eloise, who, a pack of cards in her hand, had offered to build them a card house, but she paused in her building to look at the doctor. His eyes were closed, his face calm—he really was very good-looking, but it wasn't his looks she loved, it was him. She was still looking when he opened his eyes a little so that they were mere slits and inquired: 'Why do you stare at me?'

'I don't know.' And then, her tongue getting the better of her once more: 'I quite thought that Liske would be here too.'

'I wonder why?' He sounded lazily uninterested.

'Well…' She glanced at him again very quickly; he was tickling the baby's chin and making it chuckle. 'I thought…as you were going to get married…'

'Am I? What makes you think that, Eloise?'

She snapped with a touch of peevishness: 'Nothing you've told me—you never answer any of my questions. The evidence of my own eyes, I suppose.'

His lids had drooped. 'You wish to see me married?'

She wouldn't look at him. 'Yes, if it made you happy.'

'I don't contemplate marrying for any other reason. And with half a dozen children besides?'

She added a card to her house with great care. 'Yes.'

'I hardly think that Liske would agree with you there—and it is her you have in mind as my—er—future wife?'

Eloise bit her lip, wondering how best to answer him. His voice had sounded silky and there was a note in it she didn't quite like. She was saved at the last moment by the return of the other three, who didn't come right into the room immediately but stood at the french windows, cheerfully arguing among themselves. There was time enough for her to hear the doctor say softly: 'Do you know, I have very nearly made the biggest mistake of my life, Pineapple Girl. Now I have to put it right.'

It was a pity that she had no time to ponder this remark before the other three joined them.

They stayed to dinner and she didn't speak to him alone for the rest of the evening, and on the drive back she shared the back of the car with Bluff. And when they reached Mijnheer Pringle's house, the doctor, although he came in with them, didn't stay above a couple of minutes and his goodbyes, although friendly, held nothing in them for Eloise alone.

Pieter came the next day and she wondered

afresh why such nice people as Cor and Deborah
Pringle could have had such a self-opinionated
young man for a son. He had a good deal to say
about the forthcoming trip, ate an enormous lunch,
talking about himself for most of the time, and
when later he sought her out and told her that he
was taking her out to dinner that evening, she was
very inclined to refuse. For one thing he seemed
to take it for granted that she would be overwhelmed by his attention, and for another she
didn't relish his company overmuch. But she could
see no way of refusing him without hurting his
father's feelings, and beyond an attempt, nipped in
the bud, to get Mijnheer Pringle to join them, she
could do very little about it.

Father and son wanted to talk after lunch, which
left her free to potter in the garden before engaging
Mijnheer Pringle in their daily game of chess, although this time she had Pieter breathing down the
back of her neck. She knew that he longed to ad-
vise her on every move, which made her so reckless that she lost badly. It didn't help at all when
he said heartily: 'That was bound to happen, Eloise. You should have…' He launched into a lecture
on the basic rules of the game until she was able
to escape to her room to dress.

She wasn't going to wear the grey jersey; Timon
had liked her in that. She put on the green dress

she had had for the wedding and went back to the sitting room to find the doctor, very much at his ease, standing before the fire. His 'Hullo, Eloise,' was briskly friendly and nothing more. He was staying for dinner, she was told, and he showed no signs of disappointment when he learned that she wouldn't be there; rather, he wished them a hearty goodbye, adding something about young people going out and having fun together, a remark which set her teeth on edge.

Pieter took her to a restaurant in Groningen and almost as soon as they had sat down made a fuss over the wine, so much so that the wine waiter's face assumed a wooden expression which barely concealed his contempt; it quite spoilt her dinner, although she quickly discovered that she had no need to entertain her host, since he was perfectly content to talk about himself, pausing only long enough for her to utter admiring comments. Eloise, who liked variety in her conversation, began to feel bored, although she strove to take an interest in what he was saying. But however hard she tried, it was Timon who held her thoughts.

He had gone when they got back and after sitting for half an hour with father and son, she thanked the latter prettily for her dinner, and went to bed.

It was two days before she saw the doctor again. She and Mijnheer Pringle had paid more visits, driven round the countryside, and enjoyed a visit to Franeker in order to view the planetarium. She had enjoyed that, listened carefully to the guide's careful explanation in his almost perfect English and then gone up the little staircase to study the cogs and wheels above the ceiling. It proved a good source of conversation all the way home and Mijnheer Pringle admitted that he had enjoyed it so much, they must plan another expedition as quickly as possible.

They were in fact discussing this over their dinner that evening when Doctor van Zeilst walked in. He had been out to a patient, he explained, and was on his way back to the hospital to confer with his Registrar there. He looked tired and remote, but when Mijnheer Pringle offered him coffee and something to eat, he accepted with alacrity.

The conversation was casual while he devoured soup, an omelette and the remains of one of Juffrouw Blot's desserts, but presently he sat back with a sigh while Eloise poured his coffee. 'When did you last have a meal?' she wanted to know.

'Oh, I've had a busy day—there was an accident on one of the farms very early this morning and I had a teaching round at the hospital; besides, it's the time of year when the waiting room is always full.'

'Your partners?' she prompted.

'Both away for a couple of days.'

'So when did you last have a meal?' she persisted.

'Er—an early breakfast, Eloise.' He passed his cup for more coffee, spooned in sugar lavishly and drank it with enjoyment. 'And don't look so concerned. Bart and Mevrouw Metz will be hovering with bowls of hot soup and heaven knows what else the moment I put my key in the lock.'

'I am not in the least concerned,' Eloise told him coldly, but he only grinned and began to discuss his host's trip, now only three days away. 'I'll give you a check up before you leave, Cor,' he suggested. 'You've had all the jabs you need, haven't you? Going in the afternoon are you? And you?' He had turned suddenly on Eloise. 'When do you go?'

The very thought of it made her feel sick. 'On the same day as Mijnheer Pringle—in the morning.' She left it at that.

'Plans all made? job settled?'

'No.'

'Holidays, perhaps?'

'No.'

His eyes gleamed. 'Being inquisitive and not minding my own business, aren't I?'

She looked up from the coffee cup she had been studying with all the rapt attention of one who had discovered a priceless treasure. For lack of anything more suitable, she said 'No,' once again.

'It's like trying to open a tin with a knitting needle,' he informed the room at large, and continued cheerfully: 'You must come over and say goodbye to Bart and Mevrouw Metz—Bluff as well. Let me see…not tomorrow, I think, I have a date with Liske. The day after; I'll come for you before dinner. You too, of course, Cor.'

Mijnheer Pringle smiled faintly, watching them both. 'Of course, we shall be delighted, shan't we, Eloise? Shall we have an opportunity of seeing Liske?'

Timon was at his most bland. 'I think it unlikely, but I'll convey your good wishes.' He added: 'From you both, naturally.'

He went soon after that, leaving Eloise a prey to all kinds of surmise. Why, for instance, didn't he want her to meet Liske again? It must have been apparent by now that she and Liske didn't get on, but that didn't mean to say that they couldn't spend an evening in each other's company without saying a word out of turn. Perhaps Liske didn't want to meet her again and had told him so. In a way, she decided, it was a relief to know that she had seen the last of the girl.

But that wasn't to be the case. She and Mijnheer Pringle spent the whole of the next day in the north of Groningen, lunching with the Potters and then going back home at their leisure to dine early so that Mijnheer Pringle could do his packing. He was remarkably cheerful, she was pleased to note; his lassitude and lack of interest in life around him were almost gone. True, he was an unhappy man and would be for a long time yet, but he was coming to terms with that life once more and had even talked once or twice of going back to his work as soon as he returned from Curaçao. Eloise watched him go upstairs and with a motherly injunction to call her if he needed help, took herself off to the sitting room.

She was sitting doing absolutely nothing when she heard the front door bell and Juffrouw Blot's rather heavy tread in the hall, and despite herself, she couldn't resist turning round to look at the door; there was no reason why it should be Timon. Had he not made a point about going to see Liske? All the same, her heart bounced as the door opened.

It wasn't Timon, it was Liske. She came quickly into the room and without a word of greeting demanded: 'You are alone? I wish to speak to you.'

'I'm quite alone,' said Eloise in a steady voice, and waited to hear what would come next.

Liske threw off her splendid fur coat, revealing an elegant wool dress exactly the blue of her eyes, and sat down opposite Eloise. But only for a moment; she was up and pacing round the room again so that Eloise had to turn her chair round in order to keep her in view.

'What's the matter?' she asked, determined not to let the prowling figure worry her.

'I will tell you—you have turned Timon against me, that is what is the matter! You—a silly fat girl with no looks and dowdy clothes. How dare you? But you will not succeed, do you hear? I, Liske, will not allow it. He is mine, do you understand, I wish to marry him...' She paused to take a dramatic breath ar Eloise asked quietly:

'Do you love him?'

'What has that to do with it? He has money—a great deal of it—and his lovely house and cars and an old honoured name. Besides, I wish to be his wife.'

'If he'll have you,' observed Eloise softly. 'And why on earth have you come to tell me all this? If he wants to marry you—if he loves you, do you suppose that anything I could say or do would make any difference to him? Don't be silly!'

'Silly—silly, you say!' Liske's girlish voice was shrill. 'It is you who are silly. He does not care a jot for you, you know—has he ever said so? sought you out? been attentive to you?' She paused to look into Eloise's face and went on in triumph:

'No, I can see that he has not. He is bewitched, to tell me that I mean nothing to him, that he has no wish to marry me, that I have dreamed things which he has never said...'

'And did you?' asked Eloise with interest.

Liske gave her a nasty look. 'I am a beautiful girl,' she declared with a self-assurance Eloise envied. 'If I wish for something, I have it, you understand. I shall have Timon, for I am quite beautiful and any man can be made to fall in love with me.'

'You're labouring under a misapprehension,' said Eloise, then, 'I've done nothing, nor do I intend to do anything. After all, if he had wanted me, he had only to say so, had he not? And he hasn't.'

'That I do not believe. There must be something you have done or said which has made him speak to me in this way.' Liske pounced on her coat and flung it on, looking so very beautiful that Eloise could only sit and admire her. 'I am angry,' she said loudly and quite unnecessarily, and rushed through the door, across the hall and outside to where, presumably, she had left her car.

Eloise sat where she was, her mind in a turmoil. Just what had Timon said? Had he used her as an excuse to get himself disentangled from Liske? As he had never given her any reason to suppose that he was interested in herself, she supposed so. He had made that strange remark at his sister's, that he had almost made the mistake of his life, but he could have meant anything, and nothing in his subsequent manner towards her had encouraged her to think otherwise.

She was disturbed from her rather unhappy reverie by Mijnheer Pringle calling from the landing above. 'Eloise? Who was it? Did I not hear voices?'

She got up and went into the hall. 'It was Liske. I'm not quite sure why she came; I think she's had a quarrel with Ti... Doctor van Zeilst. She went again—she's rather angry.'

He had joined her in the hall. 'She is a bad-tempered girl. It would have made Debby very happy if she had known that Timon wasn't going to marry her.'

'They are engaged, then?' She didn't care what questions she asked now; she was going so soon and afterwards it wouldn't matter.

'Certainly not. They have known each other for a long time, and it is possible that Timon has at some time or other considered her as a wife. She has so much, you see—youth and beauty and the same circle of friends—but there again,' he wrinkled his forehead in thought, 'she has so little also, no love to give to anyone but herself, no interest in his work and a great impatience with his good old Bart and Mevrouw Metz. She is also selfish and greedy; she wishes for all the good things of life and is not prepared to give anything in return. Debby never liked her, you know.'

'I don't either,' said Eloise flatly.

He gave her a perceptive look. 'No, I don't suppose you do, my dear.' They went back into the sitting room and sat down by the fire. 'It was she who upset Bart, did you know? So cruel a girl to taunt him with his age, and he a devoted servant and friend of Timon. Timon was angry about that.'

He got up and went to the cabinet where the drinks were kept. 'We will have a drink. You have had a trying evening and I am tired of packing my cases, they can wait. We will have a glass of Courvoisier, Debby always liked it.'

They sat companionably sipping their brandy and presently he said: 'Of course we go tomorrow evening as already arranged—Timon said that Liske would not be there.'

'I'm not afraid of her,' said Eloise, fired by the brandy.

'No, I don't imagine you are. Shall we wait and see? I often think that that is the best course when one is not sure what is going to happen next.' He got up and took her glass. 'Now I have some work to do in my study. Go to bed, my dear, and don't bother your head about Liske.'

So she went to bed, to dream fearful dreams of Timon waving her goodbye with Liske hanging on to his arm, wearing a fur coat and a wedding veil and laughing at her. She woke in a bad temper and didn't sleep again.

She got up in the morning with a splitting headache and the temper no better; somehow she got through the day, anxious now to get the evening over and done with; she didn't care if she didn't go, she told herself. All the same, she found herself putting on the grey jersey dress. She was sitting quietly in the sitting room, puzzling out the headlines of the *Haagsche Post*, when the doctor arrived, and although she greeted him pleasantly she made no attempt to sustain his attention and nor did he seem to wish it, embarking at once upon a conversation with Mijnheer Pringle about the weather. 'Which reminds me,' said the older man, 'talking of weather, it is just possible that I may have to return here later this evening. Pieter wanted some figures from me before we go; he was going to telephone—if he does so I've told Juffrouw Blot to let me know and I'll go back.' He paused. 'I have no car.'

'There's the Mini or the Bristol, you can borrow either, Cor,' said the doctor easily. 'A pity to spoil the evening, but if these figures are important, then you must return, of course. Are we ready?'

Bluff was in the car. Eloise got close to him and flung an arm round his woolly shoulders; he was a nice comforting creature, which was more than could be said of his master, who had barely looked at her.

The doctor's cook, his treasured Magda, had excelled herself. The table, its silver and glass winking in the soft glow of the wall sconces, was decorated with a great bowl of roses and the food was superb: if Timon wanted her to remember his home and the luxury in which he lived, thought Eloise, he had gone the right way about it. Would she ever forget the salmon mousse, the roast pheasant, the great silver dishes of vegetables, the sauces? Nor for that matter would she fail to recall the luscious bombe glacé which followed them. They had drunk champagne, but she had had only one glass; she wasn't used to it, she told her host gravely, and people said that it went to your head. He had agreed with her in the nicest possible way.

It was while they were sitting in the drawing room that the doctor was called away to the telephone and at the same time Mijnheer Pringle received a message from his own home, which left Eloise sitting alone. She curled up more comfortably in the armchair by the fire and reflected that if history were to repeat itself, Liske should make a dramatic entrance at that very moment.

Which she did. There was no ring at the door, nor was the great knocker thumped. She came in quietly, and even as Bart, crossing the hall on some errand, saw her, shut the double doors of the drawing room in his face.

One didn't need glasses to see that Liske was beside herself with rage. 'You're here—I knew it would be so! You—you harpy, you...' she paused to think, 'designing trollop!'

Eloise laughed. It was of course quite the wrong thing to do, but she couldn't help herself and it was better to do that than burst into tears or go running to Timon. She said in a reasonable voice: 'I'm not, you know. Mijnheer Pringle and I were invited to dinner, that's all.'

'Bah, I do not believe you! Where is his car if he is here, and I do not see him, nor do I believe you—you are here alone with Timon.' Her voice had risen. 'I have told him...I will not allow...'

Eloise got out of her chair. 'Oh, do be quiet,' she begged. 'How you do carry on... Timon is a man to do exactly what he wants and when he wants to do it nothing you say is going to make any difference to that. You really are a little fool.'

The other girl turned to face her across the lovely room. 'I am no fool, and that you will discover! Timon will believe anything I choose to say to him. I shall tell him…never mind that…I shall marry him also, and you can go back to England and stay there.'

Eloise wanted very much to shout back at the tiresome girl, but she managed to keep her voice low and steady. 'No, I don't think I'll do that,' she said slowly. 'I think I shall stay here and make sure that you don't have him. You are a petty, selfish girl, you deserve nothing and no one, because I don't think you have any idea what loving means. You're something under a stone…' She stopped because the look on Liske's face was pure triumph, and before she could turn her head, the girl had broken into Dutch, her voice sweet and coaxing now, and Eloise had no idea of what she was saying, although she could hear that it was eloquent and pleading and appealing.

When she did turn her head at last, Timon was there, standing by the door, leaning against the wall, his hands in his pockets. There was no expression on his face, but she knew that he was angry, although when he spoke his voice was level and quiet. 'Did you really say that, Eloise?' he asked, and when she didn't answer:

'That Liske was a trollop?' his mouth twitched a little, 'and a harpy? that she is cruel and selfish and something under a stone?'

'I said that she was something under a stone; she's got the rest wrong. I'm the harpy and the trollop…'

He ignored that. 'Why should you provoke her? She is upset, you can see that for yourself, you who are usually so sensible. And in the circumstances, that is natural enough. You should not have added to her distress, you had no need to be cruel, nor,' his voice was cold, 'did you need to interfere in my affairs—I prefer to manage them for myself.'

Eloise watched him across the room and proffer a handkerchief to Liske. She wasn't at all sure that she knew what he was talking about—why should Liske be distressed anyway? The girl was putting on a splendid show, sobbing in a picturesque manner and throwing herself into his arms. Eloise would have liked to have done that herself.

He said over his shoulder, 'You could have waited, Eloise; I would have explained, for I have a great deal to tell you, but you can see for yourself that at the moment that is impossible. Could you not have been generous?'

Eloise was standing with her mouth open, trying to understand, watching the doctor's face. Her eye caught a faint movement from Liske as he was speaking; the girl wasn't crying at all, she was smiling at her over his shoulder. Eloise felt sick. She went through the door like a breath of wind, whisked her coat from the chair where it had been cast when she had arrived, and opened the front door. To get away, and fast, was the only thought in her mind. She closed the heavy door behind her and plunged down the drive, only then realising that it was drizzling with rain and the wind was blowing a gale.

But it would have taken more than bad weather to send her back now. Let Timon console Liske; he deserved her—she swallowed tears. He hadn't minded that Liske had called her names. Perhaps he hadn't believed her; he hadn't wanted to know her side of the horrid little affair, he had even asked her to be generous. 'He's mad,' she shouted above the wind, 'and I hate him!' The strength of her feelings carried her down the drive and out into the lane.

CHAPTER EIGHT

THE WIND had become a mini-hurricane, tearing over the rolling countryside, hitting at her with giant hands, flattening her against its strength. For a moment she considered going back, but then the wind would be at her back and she would be bowled over—besides, she never wanted to see Timon again. She kept plodding on, tears, of which she was quite unconscious, pouring down her sopping cheeks. What, she asked herself, did it matter if this vile wind knocked her down, concussed her, even broke a limb—a leg or an arm, she decided, for then she would remain conscious to see Timon's remorse, although on second thoughts he wasn't likely to show remorse at all, only rage at the inconvenience, or worse than that, indifference.

She paused to gather some of the breath being bludgeoned out of her body. He had a nasty temper, but she could have managed him—she smiled a sad little smile through her tears and fought her way into the wind once more. It would be pitch dark soon; it was dark now and she felt sure that the sky she could no longer see was thunderous, but she reckoned that she was more than halfway to the main road by now and surely once there, there would be a bus. Luckily she had her purse in her coat pocket. Where she would go didn't seem important at the moment. She looked around her, although there was nothing to see by this time, just the faint glimmer of the road before her. She wasn't a nervous girl, but she had a nasty feeling that something was going to happen.

A moment later there was an uncanny lull in the wind, prelude to a flash of lightning which almost stopped her heart and a peal of thunder which crashed and banged round the wide horizon until she was deafened. And as though that wasn't enough, it began to rain in good earnest, a hard, cold deluge which soaked her in seconds. She came to a standstill; she had always hated storms, and now, alone in the dark and with no place to hide, she panicked. It was silly to shout for help, because who would hear above the howl of the returning wind and the noise of the rain? But shout she did, to no effect at all, for the wind took the sound the moment she opened her mouth. The roar of it filled her ears too, so that when she was caught roughly by the shoulders and swung round to be held fast in Timon's fierce grip, she screamed at the top of her voice. Another flash of lightning did nothing to reassure her, either; what did bring her to her senses was the vigorous shaking the doctor was giving her. She couldn't see his face, but his already strong grip became iron-fast as he turned her round again and, by the light of his torch, hurried her off the road, over a narrow stone bridge, to squelch over a muddy field which, for all she knew, might be full of fierce bulls.

She was half running in his hold, terrified out of her wits still and still finding time to marvel that he was there. Now she could stop being frightened, although from the cruel grip with which he was holding her, he was probably just as much to be frightened of as the storm. He was going at a fine pace, seemingly oblivious of the fact that Eloise was now really running to keep up with him. He seemed to know where he was going, though, as indeed she discovered very shortly when a building of some sort was lighted by his torch; she couldn't see precisely what it was; only when Timon had swung back its still solid door did she see that it had once been a cottage, a very humble one, with the thatch above their heads in a sorry state and great cracks in its walls, but still blessed shelter.

Timon banged the door shut, shone his torch around the place and then turned it on to Eloise. 'Little fool,' he said furiously, 'have you run mad? Take off that wet coat—how anyone could be so...' He muttered in Dutch and she was glad that she couldn't see his face as she meekly struggled out of the sopping garment.

There was a fireplace of sorts against one wall. He walked over to it, turned over the ash and charred wood in it with one foot and looked around him. There was wood enough; one or two broken chairs, a smashed table, a couple of boxes—Timon collected them, broke up the boxes and kindled a fire with his lighter, and without looking at Eloise once, began breaking up the wrecked table and chairs. Surprisingly, the table, once on the fire, blazed merrily, sending light if not warmth round the miserable little place, defying the violent flashes of lightning flaring at the broken window.

Eloise, out of her coat, squelched over to the fire. She was wet through to her skin, with chattering teeth and a tear-stained white face which luckily she couldn't see. She steadied her teeth long enough to say: 'How clever of you to make a fire so quickly,' and at once had her head snapped off with: 'Clever? If I were clever I would shake you until your teeth rattled!' He smiled thinly and broke a chair leg over his knee and threw it on to the fire with a force which she supposed he would have liked to have used on her, remarking silkily: 'They're rattling now, aren't they? And serve you right!'

She could only see his profile, sharp with his rage. 'How dared you?' he asked.

'It's none of your business what I dare,' she snapped. Her nerves were fiddlestrings by now and her whole shivering chest trembled with its weight of unshed tears.

He peeled off his Burberry and tossed it into a corner, taking no notice of her words at all. 'Have you any idea of the trouble you have caused? Bart is beside himself, so is Mevrouw Metz, and the maids are snivelling in corners—just because you chose to walk out into the storm for some childish reason or other.'

Her white face had gone even whiter. He had called hers a childish reason, and that meant that he didn't care at all that Liske had called her names; a designing trollop, she remembered. Perhaps he thought of her like that too. She edged a little nearer the fire and wished with all her heart that she had managed to reach the main road and was on a bus, miles away.

'Why did you come after me, then?' she asked woodenly.

He gave the fire a savage kick and said in a goaded voice: 'My dear girl, with the entire staff incapable of behaving sensibly until you were found, I had no choice.'

'Did Liske…was she worried too?'

He shot her a surprised glance. 'Liske? Surely you don't expect her to worry about you? She went home before I left the house.'

It was annoying of him not to say more, for she wanted very much to know just what had happened after she had left. She could imagine Liske weaving some pretty tale in which she was the injured, innocent party. Eloise unpinned her hair and started to wring it out in a hopeless sort of way. It really didn't matter what Timon thought of her now. Liske was determined to have him and if he was silly enough to be taken in by the wretched girl, then good luck to him. Eloise scowled horribly, choked on something which sounded very much like a small sob and said meekly: 'Oh, I see,' which meant just anything, and then asked: 'What shall we do?' She let out the ghost of a scream too at an extra vivid flash of lightning.

'Stay here, of course, until the storm has worn itself out sufficiently for us to get back.'

'Will that be long, do you think?'

'Probably all night.' They were standing side by side, steaming before the fire.

'If you want to go back,' she offered in a small voice, 'I shall be quite all right here.'

He looked down at her. 'My dear Eloise, should I return without you, I should be torn limb from limb; you seem to have cast a spell over the lot of them.' He put out a hand and touched her cheek lightly. 'Why did you have to behave as you did? Why did you have to interfere?'

She wanted to tell him that she hadn't interfered; that she hadn't behaved badly at all, but what would be the use? He was hardly likely to believe her. Oh, he would answer her courteously enough, no doubt, but she would have no chance against Liske's clever lies. And what was she supposed to be interfering about? Coming between him and Liske? Trying to turn him from her? Liske would have told him that, of course. She tried to forget the touch of his hand on her face and said crossly:

'Well, what did you expect? I have an interfering nature.'

'Yes, I know that,' he remarked surprisingly, 'but that makes no difference. But it didn't seem like you, to be unkind and ungenerous.'

He gave her a questioning look and it was on the tip of her tongue to ask him to start from the beginning and explain, but pride wouldn't let her; she stared back at him, her ordinary features screwed into defiance, so that he looked away presently, saying blandly: 'Well, for the moment there is nothing more to be said, is there? Take off your shoes and stockings and put them before the fire.'

He added, almost irritably: 'Why do you not plait your hair? It would at least be out of the way.'

She obeyed without a word and then went to pick up their coats and arrange them close to the fire before sitting down on a rickety stool he had found in some corner or other. There seemed no more to be said. She sat silent, gradually getting warm once more, and presently, her hands clasped round her knees, she let her tired head drop and dozed off.

She was awakened by his hand on her arm. His voice, calmly impersonal, pierced her brain, clouded with sleep. 'The storm's over and the wind is a great deal less. We're going back, Eloise.'

She struggled into her shoes and stockings and put on the still damp coat and tied a bedraggled scarf from its pocket over her hair without saying a word. She had no idea how long she had been asleep. Not that it mattered—really, nothing mattered. She watched him stamp out the last few embers of the fire and went with him to the door, where she discovered that the wind was only a little less than it had been, although the rain, still falling, had turned to a drizzle again. She thanked heaven that they would have the elements behind them as they returned and then winced at a pale flicker of lightning on the horizon. The doctor didn't speak at all but took her arm, and with the torch in his hand strode along, taking her with him, and big girl though she was, she had a job to keep up with him.

They seemed to walk for a long time and when they reached the lane it was almost as mushy underfoot as the field had been. But Eloise was past caring; she hardly noticed the windblown drizzle trickling down the back of her neck, her scarf was long since sodden once more, but she didn't notice that either; she was far too busy wondering what would happen next. She would be going to England in the morning, anyway, presumably under a cloud and with the memory of the doctor's anger remaining with her for the rest of her days. She had no liking for women who burst into tears for little or no reason; she told herself this as tears began to run down her cheeks; she hadn't cried so much in years, but since the gale blowing them along was quite deafening, there was no need to check them. She sobbed gently, sucking in her breath like a small child, catching the tears with the tip of her tongue and sniffing from time to time, feeling a great relief from it. By the time they reached the house she would be herself again and able to face whatever was going to happen next.

What did happen next took her quite by surprise. Her companion came to an abrupt halt, swung her round to face him and stared down at her frowningly through the dark, shouting above the wind: 'What are you crying for? You have been sniffing and sobbing for the last five minutes—I find it disturbing.'

She gave a watery snort. 'Then don't listen.'

He had produced a spotless and dry handkerchief from a pocket and begun to mop her face. 'Tomorrow,' he told her, suddenly gentle, 'we will have a talk—there is a great deal I have to say to you. You must see that being cruel to Liske was impossible. I have already been cruel enough...'

He kissed her suddenly, put the handkerchief away and walked her on once more, faster than ever. She was still gathering her wits when they turned in at the gates and started up the drive. As they rounded the curve she could see that almost every light was on in the house, and someone must have been watching for them, for the great door was open long before they reached it, with Bart on the porch and Mevrouw Metz hovering behind him.

Eloise was a little hazy after that; a great many people surrounded her, shook her hand, patted her shoulders, poured out long speeches in Dutch and took her wet things from her. They were only stopped by the doctor's voice telling her to go upstairs with Mevrouw Metz. She pulled herself together then, protesting that she had to go back to Mijnheer Pringle.

'You'll stay here, have a hot bath and go straight to bed. I'll telephone Cor now. And just for once, do as you're told, Eloise,' begged the doctor in a voice which didn't beg at all but expected to be obeyed. She was considering a retort to this when she sneezed, a signal for her to bustle up to the room where she had slept before, undressed and put into a steaming bath, clothed in a voluminous nightie of Mevrouw Metz' and popped into bed with a glass of some hot, pungent mixture which the housekeeper offered her with encouraging clucks and nods. The haziness returned after that and merged almost at once into sleep.

She awoke the next morning feeling none the worse for her adventure. True, her head ached and she had the beginnings of a sore throat, but she had no intention of telling anyone about that, and when Mevrouw Metz brought her breakfast tray, Bart, hovering discreetly in the doorway, informed her in his careful English that the doctor had gone out to an emergency case and wished her to remain where she was until he returned.

'But I'm going back to England later this morning,' she protested.

Bart nodded smilingly. 'Yes, miss, but the doctor wishes you to stay; he has, I understand, something important to discuss with you.'

No 'will you' or 'do you mind', reflected Eloise crossly. Well, she wasn't going to play doormat for anyone, and why should he wish her to stay in the first place? So that she might apologise to Liske who had been treated so cruelly? Well, she wouldn't, but to refuse point-blank wouldn't do; she had only to look at the two elderly faces looking at her so intently. 'Oh, well, in that case,' she told them airily, 'there's no more to be said, but I simply must go to Mijnheer Pringle's house and get some clothes; I've nothing fit to wear. Do you suppose I might borrow the Mini and drive over for them? I'd better go myself because I know where they are.'

She felt mean when Bart said at once that of course she was to do exactly what she wished. He would see that the car was at the door when she wanted it. 'The doctor doesn't expect to get home until late this afternoon,' he volunteered, 'there's an outbreak of food poisoning in two of the local schools and he expects to be fully occupied.'

'Nasty,' commented Eloise. 'It might take a little while to clear up, too.' And by the time it was, she would be miles away and probably forgotten.

After Mevrouw Metz and Bart had gone, Eloise gobbled down her breakfast, bathed and dressed again in her ruined clothes and went downstairs still feeling mean, although she reminded herself repeatedly that one man's poison was, in her case, her meat; it would be more than unkind to feel pleased at the outbreak of food poisoning, but it would undoubtedly keep Timon fully occupied until she was safely away. At the door, wishing Bart a guilty '*Tot ziens*,' she asked: 'Juffrouw Barrema, is she expected to call today?'

Bart gave her an inscrutable look. 'I really couldn't say, miss.' She had a feeling that he could have told her more than that, but at least she had the satisfaction of knowing that if Liske did come, she wouldn't be there to offer apologies she didn't mean.

She got into the car, waved once more to Bart, and drove quickly to Mijnheer Pringle's house.

She hadn't stopped to consider what she would say to that gentleman when she saw him, and she was spared that worry by finding him from home. Juffrouw Blot, made aware by some means or other of her last night's adventure, found nothing strange in Eloise's awkwardly expressed statement that she was returning to England at once, for she had known that she would be leaving on the same day as Mijnheer Pringle. She went away to fetch Eloise's case and then to make coffee while Eloise tore into another dress and coat, quite frightened

that Timon might have returned home unexpectedly and be even now on his way to fetch her back.

The taxi she had asked Juffrouw Blot to get was
at the door by the time she got downstairs; she
scribbled a hasty note to Mijnheer Pringle, wishing
him goodbye and a pleasant trip, aware that it was
quite inadequate but unable to think of anything
better, exchanged a warm embrace with Juffrouw
Blot, and jumped into the taxi.

It wasn't until they were in the crowded streets
of Groningen that she began to feel safe. She paid
off the taxi at the station and bought herself a ticket
to Schiphol. The fare was quite frightening, but she
paid it recklessly, telling herself that it was a small
price to pay for getting away so easily and ignoring
the small voice at the back of her head telling her
persistently that she didn't want to get away at
all—never to see Timon again, to have to think of
him married to Liske; she would make him a terrible wife... She stood on the platform waiting for
the train and wished she were anywhere else but
where she was.

She had plenty of time for reflection once she
was in the train; it was a quite lengthy journey and
once at Amsterdam she had to find her way to the
KLM terminal and board the bus for Schiphol and
once there arrange a transfer to an earlier flight;
the one she had booked wasn't due out for another

two hours, too long a time to wait. She toyed with the idea of telephoning Mijnheer Pringle and dismissed it. He would only tell Timon and the whole object of her flight, to disappear decently with no fuss, would be defeated. She would write when she got back to the hospital; she had the address in Curaçao. She sat through the short flight with an empty mind which refused to cope with any plans for the future, it was enough that she had returned without difficulty. She closed her eyes and tried to sleep but instead found herself thinking of Timon.

She was expected at St Goth's, that at least made life more normal; she went to her room and put away her things and sat down to decide what to do. Her application form, already filled in, was in the drawer where she had left it; she supposed that she should go at once to Miss Dean's office and hand it in. It was really a little awkward; she was actually no longer on the staff even though she had been allowed a room until she returned from Holland. Presumably if she got the Sister's post, she would be given a bedsitter in the Sisters' Wing. The prospect left her indifferent; a secure future, a chance to climb to the top of the nursing profession, a steady income with a pension at the end of it…anything but that!

She went downstairs and asked for an appointment with Miss Dean early the next morning and presently went to supper, where she ate nothing at all, pushing the food round her plate while she answered her friends' questions about her stay in Holland. She telephoned her mother later, telling her almost nothing, allowing her to believe that she would accept the post of Night Sister if she should be offered it. Time enough to let her know her plans for the future when she knew them herself. She then went to bed and cried herself to sleep.

She got up in the morning resolved not to shed another tear, and made her way to Miss Dean's office. That lady received her kindly, inquired after Mijnheer Pringle's health, hoped that Doctor van Zeilst had been satisfied with her services as a nurse and then waited, hands clasped before her on her desk, for Eloise to speak.

She could have been no more surprised at Eloise's next words than Eloise herself; she heard her own voice, quite calm and unhurried, telling her superior that she had decided against applying for the Night Sister's post, indeed, against hospital work of any sort, at least for the time being, and as this decision had only at that very moment entered her head, even though she had known since the night before that she wasn't going to apply for the job, she could only gape when Miss Dean inquired with well-concealed surprise if she had any idea what she was going to do.

Eloise uttered the first thing which entered her head. 'I want to go a long way away,' she stated clearly, 'and look after children or babies—but it would have to be in the country.'

Miss Dean, a practical woman even when confronted by the unlikely situation of one of her most promising nurses apparently without her wits, answered immediately: 'In that case, Staff Nurse, since you are not technically on the staff, I am free to make a suggestion. Should you wish for a temporary post while you reconsider your position, I may be able to help you. My brother is headmaster of a boys' prep school in Cumbria—near Buttermere, but rather remote. He telephoned me only yesterday and mentioned that the school matron had a nasty attack of shingles and was desperate for a substitute. About two or three weeks, I believe, probably less. If you are interested, I could recommend you.'

'I should like that,' said Eloise without stopping to think about it. 'It's just what I want.'

Miss Dean reached for the telephone. 'And of course,' she went on smoothly, 'if you feel differently at the end of your stay there, I will consider your application to rejoin the nursing staff. It would have to be as a staff nurse, you understand, but there will be other Sisters' posts.'

Eloise said: 'Yes, Miss Dean,' but she wasn't

really listening. Cumbria was a long way off and no one would know that she was there. By no one she meant Timon, of course; not that he would want to know, although it would be wonderful if… She came back to her surroundings with a jerk to find Miss Dean speaking on the telephone and looking at her in a questioning manner. 'I asked,' said that lady patiently, 'if you could travel up there today? There is a train about noon and you would have to change at Lancaster for Keswick where you will be met—there is a car journey of half an hour from there. Your expenses will be paid and you will receive a salary *pro rata*.'

'That will do nicely.' Eloise watched her boats burning behind her and didn't care at all.

Miss Dean spoke into the telephone, put down the receiver, asked: 'You have enough money, Staff Nurse?' and when Eloise said yes, she had: 'Then I suggest that you go and pack a few things for your new job.' She smiled nicely. 'And I hope to see you again shortly.'

Eloise said: 'Yes, Miss Dean,' which could have meant anything, and wasted no time; there was her mother to telephone, there was a case to pack and the warden to see about her room; she should by rights give it up instanter, but since Miss Dean had left a loophole for her, surely she would be allowed to keep it for another week or two, in case she came back. But she wouldn't do that, she knew that for certain now; she would have to find a job as far away from London as possible, something which would keep her so busy that she would have little time to remember. She told herself bracingly to be thankful that things had turned out so well, gave her mother the bare bones of the matter in an over-bright voice which disturbed her parent very much, packed a case with suitable clothes for the Lake District in early winter, bade brief goodbyes to such of her friends as she could conveniently find, and took a taxi to the station.

The journey was uneventful, but throughout its length she didn't allow herself to think deeply; she speculated on the job ahead, took a close interest in the scenery, and read several newspapers from cover to cover without taking in a single word. It was a relief to reach Lancaster at last and catch the local train to Keswick. The country was worth looking at now, and Keswick, when she reached it, looked charming. She got out of the train eagerly, anxious to get the journey finished with now, for it seemed hours since she had left London and it was as though she were in a different country. There weren't many people on the platform and she spotted the man who had been sent to meet her almost at once—one of the housemasters, Miss Dean had told her, and here he was, looking the

part; tall and thin and stooping. Just for a moment
she thought she had been mistaken, though, for he
stood lost in thought, not looking about him at all,
but then, apparently remembering where he was,
he gazed around him, saw her and came at once,
peering at her through pebble glasses.

'Miss Bennett? Ah—welcome. I'm Carter—
John Carter. You have no idea how glad we shall
all be to have you with us—our Miss Maggs is laid
low and we are lost, completely lost without her.'

If they were all like him, thought Eloise, that
seemed very likely. She wished him a brisk how
do you do, exchanged a few banalities about the
journey and accompanied him outside the station
to where a Landrover was drawn up to the kerb.

Mr Carter put her case in the back and opened
the door for her to get in beside him. 'The school's
rather remote,' he explained, and set off at a pace
which rattled the teeth in her head.

They left the town behind them quickly enough,
taking a road which led them through the hills,
already only dimly to be seen in the dusk, and after
the first mile or so Eloise quite saw why Mr Carter
drove a Landrover, for they turned off on to a side
road presently, which dipped and twisted over
rough ground, its own surface none too smooth.
Mr Carter drove badly, with the manner of a man
who hated doing it, any way and he spoke little,

answering Eloise's questions with a minimum of words, so that presently she gave up trying to hold a conversation with him and sat staring into the dark, wishing that it was Timon sitting beside her.

It was a relief when they arrived at a very small village and her companion stated: 'The school is another mile along this road—there's a drive on our left.'

As indeed there was, marked by two very small lodges, built apparently for dwarfs. The drive ran, straight as a ruler, to the imposing pile of the school, standing well back from the road, lights shining from its windows. Eloise, who was hungry, was glad to see it at last.

Mr Carter drove round to a side door, stopped the Landrover with a frightful jolt, took her case inside, muttered something about putting the car away, gave a great shout for someone called Mrs Emmett, and went away, leaving Eloise standing uncertainly in a gloomy passage wondering what to do. She didn't have long to wait, however. A small, round woman with grey hair and pale blue eyes appeared through a door, talking as she came. 'You'll be the new matron—you'll want a meal and see your room, I'll be bound.' She picked up the case and opened another door for Eloise to go through. There was a staircase in front of them, and with Mrs Emmett toiling ahead of her, Eloise went up it, heartened by the thought of supper. Her room was close by the stairs, and comfortable enough with a small electric fire and an armchair drawn up close to it.

'Bathroom's down the passage,' Mrs Emmett told her, 'supper's in half an hour; I'll be back for you in twenty minutes so's you can see the head-master first.' She smiled and trotted off, leaving Eloise disappointed; she would have liked a cup of tea, but it seemed she wasn't going to get one, so she explored her room, unpacked her case, in-spected the white uniform and little caps someone had thoughtfully provided for her use, did her hair and face and sat down to wait for Mrs Emmett.

'You're the housekeeper?' she inquired when that lady reappeared.

'Yes, Matron—and a busy woman I am, too. If you would just come with me, Dr Dean will see you now.'

They went back the way they had come and down another passage which brought them out into the main hall where the housekeeper tapped on a door, opened it, gave Eloise's name, and disap-peared, leaving Eloise to get herself into the room and cross its vast carpet to the desk where the headmaster was standing.

He looked stern, but perhaps he had to because of the boys in his care, but he wasn't as old as she had expected, although a beard did add to his age. He greeted her in a no-nonsense fashion, thanked her for stepping into the breach, begged her to take a chair and gave her, very briskly, a résumé of the tasks which she would be expected to perform.

'You have had no experience of school nursing?' he wanted to know. 'Miss Maggs, our regular Matron, has of course spent a lifetime at it and is naturally an expert at her work.'

And she would need to be, Eloise fancied, if she performed half the jobs the headmaster had rattled off so glibly. He resumed: 'This is only a temporary post, as you know. We hope that Miss Maggs will be back before long. Meanwhile, we are very grateful to you for filling in for her.'

It was obvious that these gracious words marked the end of the interview. Eloise got to her feet and he marched to the door beside her and opened it, saying: 'Please feel free to come to me if there are any problems.'

There were dozens, and the most pressing one was where did she go for her supper. She was standing in the hall wondering which door to open when a youngish man came into the hall. 'Lost?' he asked. 'You're the temporary Matron, aren't you? Come with me and I'll show you where we have supper—with the boys, I'm afraid, but don't let that affect your appetite.'

Nothing would affect it. She followed her guide along a long passage to double doors which opened on to the dining hall, a vast, lofty place and very draughty. It was filled with long tables, lying parallel to each other and presided over, as it were, by another table raised on a platform at one end of the hall. Evidently this was where the staff sat; she could see Mr Carter standing behind a chair, looking down at the boys waiting to sit, presumably when he said so. Her companion hurried her along, introduced her to such of the staff who were within speaking distance, indicated a chair and went to stand at his own chair. Mr Carter must have been waiting for them, for he said a lengthy grace and everyone sat down. Eloise, sitting between two learned, grey-haired gentlemen, found herself facing the boys below her; there seemed to be an awful lot of them; she had forgotten to ask how many—some of them seemed quite small and she supposed that they sat in houses, for at the top and bottom of each table there were older boys sitting, but she didn't waste much time on speculation; a maid was bringing round plates of soup and that interested her far more.

Supper was a substantial meal and she enjoyed it, as she enjoyed the conversation of her neighbours. They all stood through another long grace, in Latin this time, and with her original guide to show her the way, went back to her room. 'There's no one sick at the moment,' he told her, 'but if you'd like to go to the end of this passage you'll find the sick bay; it might help if you were to explore it.' He grinned at her. 'My name's Sewell, by the way, Dick Sewell.'

'And mine's Eloise Bennett—thanks for showing me around.' She bade him goodnight, and did as he suggested, to discover that the sick bay was ten-bedded, well equipped and cheerful. There was a small treatment room leading from it as well as an isolation ward with one bed in it. She pottered round for half an hour or more, discovering where everything was, and on her way back to her room met Mrs Emmett.

'Miss Maggs and me usually have a cup of tea about now,' said the housekeeper pleasantly. 'I wondered if you would like one with me?'

'Oh, please—and perhaps you could tell me one or two things—what time to get up and if there's a sick parade, and do I go to the hall for breakfast…'

'We'll go to my room, Matron, and have a little chat.' Mrs Emmett led the way downstairs and ushered Eloise into her own sitting room, crowded with old-fashioned furniture and with a great many photos in frames arranged on every available surface, but it was homelike and the tea was hot and

strong and there were biscuits with it. Eloise sat
by the old-fashioned fireplace and toasted her feet
while her companion gave her a bird's eye view
of what her day would be. A long one, by all accounts, starting at half past seven in the morning
and ending after supper, and taking in the checking
of the laundry, the inspection of the boys' clothes,
the sick parade, the attending to any minor injuries
and the care of any boy in the sick bay. Eloise went
to bed presently, trying to remember everything
she had been told, all the same, it was of Timon
she was thinking when she finally went to sleep.

She got through her first day's work very well.
There were several boys with cut fingers, chil-
blains, sore throats and boils, but once she had
dealt with them she was free to work her way
through the laundry, piled high and not attended to
since the unfortunate Miss Maggs had been carried
off sick. She inspected the dormitories too, a little
vague as to what was expected of her, and after
lunch she had an hour or two to herself. It was a
clear, chilly day, so she wrapped herself up warm
and went for a brisk walk down to the village
where she bought a few odds and ends at the only
shop and then telephoned her mother.

Mrs Bennett sounded worried. 'It sounds a long
way away,' she observed. 'Is it hard to find, darling?'

Eloise told her and then extolled the scenery, the size of the school and the comfort of her room, and finally her mother observed: 'Well, dear, it sounds quite nice. Are you going back to St Goth's?'

'No—I don't know. I—I thought I'd make up my mind while I'm here.' And with that her mother had to be content.

The days passed quickly enough. There was plenty to do but none of the work was arduous, and after a little while Eloise began to get to know the boys, the little ones especially. Privately she considered that an eight-year-old was too young to send away from home and judging from the number she discovered were homesick, she thought that quite likely she was right. There was a certain amount of bullying, of course, and at least once a day, a fight about something or other, but as various masters hastened to assure her, boys would be boys and they had to expend their energy on something or someone, and they were taught to fight fair. She quickly learned to deal with a black eye or bruised knuckles without asking too many questions, although it seemed to her that one or two of the boys came off worst every time. One especially, an undersized, spectacled boy of eight or nine years, Smith Secundus by name, for he had a much older brother in the school. Eloise came across him on several occasions getting roughed up with what she considered to be quite unnecessary violence, so much so that on one particular morning she had waded in to rescue him and taken the names of the three much older boys who were plaguing him—Tomkins, Mallory and Preedy, they had told her rather defiantly, and had refused to tell her why they so frequently set about Smith Secundus.

'Well, I shall find out,' she told them sternly, 'and if it doesn't stop I shall see your housemasters about it. Smith Secundus, come to the treatment room and have that nose-bleed dealt with.' She had marched him away and done her best to worm out of him why he was so unpopular.

He told her finally, his voice muffled against the cold compress she was holding to his small nose. 'They don't like me because I'm small and I like lessons.' He added proudly: 'I'm very good at maths, Matron.'

Eloise gave him a comfortable pat. 'Good for you, and you'll grow, my dear, and in a little while when they understand maths too, you'll all be friends and laugh about it.'

He hadn't believed her. 'I shall do something desperate,' he had told her rather importantly as she had tidied him up and sent him back to his class.

CHAPTER NINE

ELOISE KEPT an eye on Smith Secundus for the next day or two, but he seemed to have settled down; at least she saw no signs of bullying, and any fighting there was was the cheerful give and take of boys enjoying a rough-house together. She had become quite fond of them all, although she wasn't sure if she could manage the older boys, who tended to regard her as someone of their own age. All the same, she had settled down during the two weeks in which she had been there, and if she wasn't happy, at least she was learning to live with the prospects of never seeing Timon again. She resolutely stopped herself from thinking about him and that made her feel empty and sad, but that, she felt sure, would pass in time, and in the meantime she must make up her mind what she wanted to do once the school no longer needed her.

Miss Maggs had returned that very morning, and Eloise realised anxiously that she had really made no plans at all. Her mother wanted her to go home for a holiday and she was tempted to do that, although it wouldn't solve her problem. Perhaps she should go back to St Goth's after all, and supposing she did? What if Timon should turn up one day? After all, Sir Arthur Newman was a friend of his—it would be like turning a knife in a wound if she had to see him again. She thought about it until her head ached, and came to no conclusion at all.

She finished her work earlier than usual that afternoon and Miss Maggs was closeted with the headmaster. It was a fine, cold day, with a decided nip in the air; she got her coat and started off for a walk; exercise was what she needed. She went a long way and the afternoon was failing as she took the little path which ran alongside the drive. The school looked rather spectacular from where she was, the fading light warming its stone walls. She stopped to admire it—and then suddenly began to run towards it. There was someone on the balustrade which ran right round the attic floor of the house, standing out on the narrow ledge between the sewing room and the attic where the luggage was stored. She knew who it was, too—small and black-haired and rigid. Smith Secundus.

She ran well and she made light of the stairs to the top of the house. The sewing room door was open and she made herself slow down and go in quietly, taking off her coat as she went. At the open window she leaned out. 'Hullo,' she said cheerfully, 'what are you doing out there?'

His voice came to her in a whisper. 'They called me a dwarf—they said I wouldn't grow—Mallory and Preedy and Tomkins…I'll make them sorry…' Eloise could hear the rising hysteria in the treble voice and stretched herself a little further out of the window. 'I'll jump,' said Smith Secundus.

'Well, yes, dear,' she spoke soothingly, 'but that wouldn't be of much use, would it? I mean, the boys would get a nasty shock if you did, but what would be the point of that if you weren't there to see?' She swung a shapely leg over the sill and tried not to look down to the ground far below. 'It would be a frightful waste.'

She saw that the good sense of this remark had struck him and added in a voice which shook only very slightly with fright: 'I'll come out on to the ledge with you and stretch out my hand—I think you'll be able to reach it and catch hold, then you can edge back…'

He turned a face stiff with terror towards her. 'I can't—Matron, I can't. I'm going to fall.'

'Of course you can, Smith Secundus.' Eloise spoke with brisk authority, but her heart sank as she saw that the rest of him was stiff with terror too. He looked as though he were carved in stone and just as hard to budge.

'I'm going to fall,' he repeated.

'Pooh, don't be silly!' She was still brisk, quite

sure that she would fall herself before very long; heights had never been her strong suit, but it was not time to be worrying about that. She swung the other leg over the sill as she spoke, murmuring vague prayers as she did so, and stood upright on the ledge, a hand clutching at the parapet behind her. Gingerly she turned until her back was pressed hard against it, one hand still clinging to it as though she would have soldered it there, the other stretched out to the boy. There was still a gap between them and she moved sideways, refusing to allow her mind to dwell on the fact that the ledge was barely a foot wide.

'Catch hold,' she told Smith Secundus, 'and come towards me, my lamb—sideways like a crab, and don't look down. We'll go back together.'

It sounded easy and she was proud of her steady voice even though she was silently screaming her head off for help. And that was futile, she knew; the boys would be back from their paperchase by now and in the dressing rooms behind the gym changing their clothes and making more than enough noise to drown a dozen screams. There was no help.

There was. Her terrified eyes, much against her will, had looked down; coming up the drive with smooth soundlessness was a silver-grey Rolls-Royce. It stopped precisely outside the entrance a little to her left and Timon van Zeilst got out. Even from that distance and angle he looked reassuringly large; the epitome of security. Eloise whispered his name and then, in a remarkably squeaky voice, shouted it. He was already strolling towards the porch, but he stopped and looked up, saw them at once and then before she could get another sound out of her dry mouth, disappeared inside.

The minute that passed seemed like a year; Smith Secundus was crying now and his hand felt cold and clammy in hers. She had pulled her gaze away from the ground once more and was concentrating on clinging to the parapet with all her strength—they only had to hang on a little longer...

Without turning her head, for she dared not, she knew that Timon was at the window, one leg, indeed, already over its sill. His voice, reassuringly matter-of-fact, sounded quite placid. 'Boy—you'll do exactly as I say. Step sideways towards Eloise, and when I tell you, step past her—there's room enough if you press close to her. You'll be perfectly safe; she's holding you and I'm holding her.'

Eloise felt his large firm grasp round her hand and its reassuring squeeze and heard, incredibly, his laugh, and Smith Secundus said in a wobbly voice: 'Yes, sir—but it's Matron, sir.'

'Is that what they call you, Pineapple Girl? Anyone less matronly…' His voice became brisk and commanding once more. 'Now boy, come along.' And Smith Secundus came, with a heart-stopping stumble or two, pressing his bony little body against Eloise so that her bones ached with the effort to keep steady while he wormed his way past her. After what seemed an age she heard the doctor say: 'Good man—very nicely done. Over the sill with you and into a chair, and stay in it. You can leave go of my hand now.'

Eloise felt his hand tighten on hers. 'And now, my pretty, you'll do the same—it will be easier this time; you're nearer and I'm right here beside you. All you have to do is move sideways—don't look down and don't hurry.'

'I'm so much bigger,' she pointed out shakily.

'And so much braver—and not so big that I can't hang on to you easily enough with one hand if I have to. Come on.'

She was too scared to do anything else—indeed, she was beyond thinking for herself any more. With a few cautious, terrified steps she found herself beside the doctor's reassuring bulk and then whisked with surprising strength across him and tossed through the window. She landed untidily on the window seat and was barely on her feet when he was beside her.

'My poor girl,' he said in a kind voice, and

caught her close. She looked up into his face and was surprised to see how white and drawn and somehow older it was. 'Timon, oh, Timon!' she mumbled, and heaven knew what she might have said if he hadn't released her almost at once and said in a matter-of-fact voice: 'You both need a cup of tea. Is there anyone…?'

Eloise did her best to sound as matter-of-fact as he did. 'Yes, there's Miss Maggs, she's the School Matron—she came back today, actually I was on my way to have tea with her when I saw… Smith could come with me…' She looked anxiously at him. 'We don't need to say anything, do we?'

He stared at her thoughtfully, sat her down in a chair and went to sit on the arm of the boy's chair. 'I came to see the headmaster about another matter—I think I could explain to him—he will have to know.' He put out a hand and ruffled Smith Secundus's untidy hair. 'Don't worry, boy, we'll get it sorted out. And you, Eloise—er—Matron, could you explain over the tea-cups; the lad can fill in the gaps.' He looked down at the boy. 'Why did you do it, Smith?'

It all came pouring out once more while the doctor listened gravely and then remarked simply: 'We all do silly things now and then. I shouldn't think anyone need know other than the headmaster and your housemaster—and the lady Matrons, of course.' He grinned suddenly at Eloise, who frowned.

Unimpressed by the severity of her expression, he got to his feet. 'Shall we go, then?'

Eloise went to the mirror above the old-fashioned grate and straightened her sadly battered cap. It was heaven to see him again, but he needn't suppose that she was going to behave like a meek doormat... She took her time and, her headgear once more arranged to her satisfaction, asked: 'Why are you here?'

He looked wicked. 'Interested? I seem to remember you saying that you didn't care if you never saw me again.'

'Well, and I don't.' She spoke mendaciously and much too quickly.

'Your mother seemed to think otherwise.'

'Mother?' She stared at him round-eyed. 'She's not here?'

'At Eddlescombe. I went there after I had been to St Goth's—looking for you, Eloise.'

She had gone to stand by the boy, putting a comforting arm round his narrow shoulders. 'Why?'

'That will have to wait for the moment. Supposing we go, as I suggested, and find Miss Maggs.'

The School Matron was sitting at a small table in her neat sitting room, carefully repairing some small boy's coat. If she was surprised to see a very large man open the door in answer to her 'Come in', and stand aside to allow her colleague and Smith Secundus to enter, she didn't betray it. She smiled at Eloise, gave the boy a quick, all-seeing glance and turned her attention to her visitor.

'Doctor van Zeilst,' said Eloise breathlessly.

Miss Maggs' blue eyes twinkled nicely at him. 'Ah, yes, of course,' she murmured in a pleased way, 'the headmaster did mention...' They exchanged a look and she went on smoothly: 'Will you join us for tea?'

'Thank you, no, Matron—I have an appointment with Dr Dean and I believe that I am already a little late.' Timon turned round to look at Eloise. 'And you, Matron, could perhaps discuss what is best to be done while you have your tea.' He smiled suddenly. '*Tot ziens*, dear girl.' He shook hands with Miss Maggs, ruffled the boy's hair once more and at the door turned to say: 'They had rather a nasty experience, Miss Maggs, but I'm sure that I leave them in excellent hands.'

He had gone. Eloise stared at the gently shutting door, unable to believe that he could have walked off in such a casual manner; without even bothering to inquire how she—or Smith Secundus, for that matter—felt. She frowned fiercely to check the tears she would have liked to shed and said too brightly: 'Well, that's done and finished with—we'll feel fine when we've had a cup of tea.'

Miss Maggs was a wise woman; she looked at the boy's white face and Eloise's cross one and allowed them to drink two cups of tea and empty the bread and butter plate before she interrupted her gentle flow of small talk to ask: 'An old friend of yours, my dear?'

Eloise went bright pink. 'No—yes, that is we knew each other just for a little while in Holland.'

Miss Maggs nodded her severely coiffed head. 'And he came all this way to see you. I have been wondering why a nice girl like you should wish to bury yourself in such a remote part. Still, he's found you now.'

'He wasn't looking for me,' said Eloise gruffly, 'he's going to marry a Dutch girl—she's fair and slim...' She glanced down at her nicely rounded person and sighed.

Miss Maggs remained unruffled by this statement. 'There's many a slip...' she quoted mildly. She was a woman who liked her proverbs, and what was more, believed in them, too.

'Timon doesn't make slips,' declared Eloise gloomily, and Smith Secundus, who had been allowed to get up from the table and look at Miss Maggs' photograph album of old boys, said unexpectedly: 'No, he didn't, did he, Matron? He walked along the ledge just as though he was on the ground and he felt like a great big tree. Why does he speak English if he comes from Holland?'

'He's a very well educated man,' supplied Eloise gloomily. 'And now we'd better tell Miss Maggs all about it, hadn't we—right from the beginning.'

Miss Maggs, her placid face set in comfortable attentiveness, listened, popping in a question here and there when Smith Secundus got too involved or excited and saying at the end of their joint recital: 'Well, Smith, it was a foolish thing to do, wasn't it? How fortunate Matron was close at hand and brave enough to come to your rescue, or you might still have been out there, catching dear knows what kind of a cold. I hope you intend to thank her properly for coming to your aid, and as for the doctor who rescued you, nothing less than a letter of thanks in your best handwriting will do.'

'Shall I have to see Dr Dean?' asked the boy unhappily.

'Naturally, and so will Matron, but as to punishment I imagine that he will consider that you have had enough of that, standing out there on that nasty ledge. There's no more to be said about it now; I'm only thankful that it didn't turn out worse than it was. You'll go to bed after you have seen the headmaster and I shall come and take a look at you later, just to make sure that you're all right...' She was interrupted by a knock on the door and the entrance of one of the school prefects. Eloise was required in Dr Dean's study, and Smith Secundus was to go to his housemaster's room.

Eloise put up a hand to tuck away a stray end of hair. Her appearance wasn't as pristine as she could have wished, but really that hardly mattered. She got to her feet, caught sight of the look of dread on the small Smith's face and said bracingly: 'We'll come at once, thank you—don't wait; I'll take Smith Secundus along as I go.'

There was no one about in the long corridor outside Matron's room. Eloise took her small companion's hand and when they reached his housemaster's room, knocked on the door and went in with him.

Mr Sewell, the housemaster, was standing before the gas fire, warming himself, and he turned a stern face to them as they entered.

'Thank you, Matron—it is Smith Secundus I wish to see.'

'Oh, I know that,' agreed Eloise, who hadn't quite learned how to be a school Matron. 'I just popped in to warn you that this boy has had a very nasty fright. He was very good and brave though, once he saw how silly he'd been. I'd be proud of him if he were my son.' She smiled warmly at the glowering housemaster. 'I shouldn't be surprised if he doesn't grow up to be a fine man,' she assured him, and then to the boy: 'You have no need to be afraid now; Mr Sewell is going to explain just how silly you were, my dear, but you don't need to be afraid of him, and if you're punished, mind you take it like a man. I'll see you at supper.'

She smiled warmly at them both and Mr Sewell actually smiled back.

The headmaster looked stern too, but not frighteningly so. He offered her a chair and said without preamble: 'Doctor van Zeilst has told me about this unfortunate incident, Matron...' He paused and Eloise glanced quickly round the room. Timon wasn't there and she was aware of bitter disappointment, although there was no reason why she should; he had shown a lamentable lack of interest in her. She swallowed the knot of tears which had been in her throat ever since she had climbed on to that awful ledge, and gave her attention to the learned gentleman addressing her.

'I must thank you, Matron, for your presence of mind and courage—it could have been a serious accident, even tragedy. After discussion it has been agreed that the boy has been sufficiently punished, and I hope that you concur. I shall of course speak very severely to those boys who caused him to take such a drastic course.'

'Good—I detest bullies, and he's only a little boy and he showed plenty of pluck.'

'So Doctor van Zeilst assured me.'

She couldn't resist asking: 'He's a friend of yours, Headmaster? I mean, it seemed so strange to see him here, it's rather off the beaten track…'

'So he himself observed. No, Matron, I have not had the pleasure of meeting the doctor before. A fine man, if I may say so.'

She hoped that he was going to say more than that, and looked at him encouragingly, but he merely smiled, remarked that he didn't wish to detain her and got to his feet once more, a sign that the interview was over.

There was plenty to keep her busy that evening. She had supper with Miss Maggs, who didn't mention the doctor once but talked a great deal about Eloise's departure, something Eloise didn't much want to discuss. Once she had left the school she would have severed the last slender link with Timon—a good thing; general opinion had always had it that a clean break was the thing. But it wasn't. She had done that once and what good had it done? The moment she had set eyes on Timon getting out of his car she had come alive again.

She sorted sheets after supper, dosed one or two boys with colds, peeped in on the sleeping Smith Secundus and took herself off to bed, where she was at last able to cry her eyes out in peace and quiet.

She was to leave, it was decided in the morning, in two days' time. Everyone had been very nice, had praised her lavishly for her part in rescuing Smith Secundus, wished her a pleasant future, and beyond Miss Maggs, had shown no further interest. That lady, however, made up for that by displaying a lively curiosity as to where she would go. 'I know you came here on a temporary basis,' she observed, 'and of course, it's none of my business, but have you another post to go to?'

Eloise shook her head. 'Well, no—I thought perhaps I'd have a short holiday and then perhaps go abroad for a while.'

Her companion gave her a shrewd look and said nothing to this, so Eloise felt bound to add: 'I've always thought I should like to…'

'Australia?' queried Miss Maggs, 'it's a long way away, but I hear from all counts that there are excellent prospects there. You hadn't thought of getting married, I suppose?'

Eloise gave her a goaded glare; she had thought of nothing else, quite pointlessly, for some weeks now. 'No, I haven't.' She put down the neat pile of shirts she had been folding. 'Shall I go along and take young Adams' temperature? He looked feverish to me this morning when he reported a cold—I thought I'd look him over for spots.'

'A sensible suggestion,' agreed her senior, 'half term, you know, a week or so ago, and if there's anything catching about, you may be sure one of the boys will bring it back with him.'

Adams, a small, plump boy with spiky hair and round blue eyes, had a temperature, he had spots, too. Eloise cast a professional eye over him, reported her findings to Miss Maggs with the observation that it looked like chickenpox to her, and set about transferring the patient to the isolation ward and telephoning the school doctor.

The rest of the day was nicely taken up with this exercise and the careful scrutiny of any small boys who had been in contact with the victim; there were any number of them, but they all looked, for the moment at least, remarkably healthy. Miss Maggs, over their evening cup of tea, expressed the fervent hope that Adams would be the only case, and that a light one.

He was well covered in spots by the following morning and a little pale and lethargic, but Doctor Blake pronounced himself quite satisfied with him, and left Eloise to make the boy comfortable for the day, observing as he went: 'I hear that you are leaving us, Matron—I'm sure we shall all be sorry to lose you. I believe Miss Maggs has arranged for a nurse to take over tomorrow, if you would be good enough to keep an eye on him today.'

Eloise didn't believe in beating about the bush; she went straight to Miss Maggs and asked: 'Why don't you want me to stay on, Miss Maggs? You know I haven't a job to go to. I could have easily stayed another week, or at least until Adams is better, it would have made no difference.'

The Matron looked uncomfortable. 'Well, dear, nothing would have pleased me more, but Dr Dean told me quite positively that arrangements had already been made and that you were to be free to go in the morning. In fact, I hear the nurse is arriving this afternoon, directly after lunch.'

Eloise felt quite bewildered. 'Is she? But why…?' and then, suddenly rather cross: 'In that case she can take over straight away; it won't take me a minute to pack and I can leave this afternoon just as easily as tomorrow. In fact, I could go now—this minute…'

Miss Maggs looked, if that were possible, even more uncomfortable. 'Oh, I'm not sure…'

'Well, I am. Someone could have told me—all this secrecy—if they want me away why didn't they say so? Wild horses wouldn't keep me here. For two pins I'd walk out this very minute!'

Her superior's agitation was quite alarming. 'Oh, my dear, don't do that—at least…' She glanced at the clock. 'If you could just change Adams' bed for him first—it wouldn't take more than half an hour—and there are all those sheets and pillow-cases... I'd do it, but I've all these forms to see to.'

Eloise was cross and hurt, but neither of these feelings had been caused by Miss Maggs. 'Yes, of course I'll do that,' she promised, and put down her coffee cup. 'All the same, I shall go just as soon as the nurse arrives.'

Miss Maggs made a soothing sound and looked at the clock again and when Eloise had taken her-self off, allowed herself a sigh of relief.

Eloise had Adams sitting in a chair, wrapped in a blanket, and was smoothing the bottom sheet, when the door opened and Timon came in. At the sight of him her heart missed a beat, turned over and leapt into her throat so that the only sound she could manage was a small choking breath.

'Hullo,' said Timon, and smiled at her.

The smile played even more havoc with her heart, but she ignored that. 'Have you had the chickenpox?' she demanded in a severe voice. 'This boy's in isolation.'

He had strolled right into the little room, to lean against a wall and watch her. 'I have indeed, abun-dantly, at the age of six.'

She had a sudden vivid picture of a small spotty

Timon, probably refusing to stay in bed; he would have been a lively small boy... 'Oh, well— Have you lost your way? Did you come to see the headmaster again?'

'I came to see you, Eloise.'

Her heart did a somersault, but she replied coldly. 'That's too bad; I'm leaving in about half an hour.'

His eyebrows rose. 'Indeed? I understood you to be going tomorrow morning.'

She began: 'Well, I...' and then: 'How did you know that?' She mitred the corners of the top blanket very precisely and invited the spotty Adams to jump back into bed.

'Oh, I arranged it with the headmaster.' His voice was bland. 'Miss Maggs, however, had the good sense to telephone me and tell me your change of plans.'

'You arranged it...you must be joking... I've never heard...' She stopped to draw an indignant breath.

'No, dear girl, I don't joke about it; I don't joke about something which matters to me more than anything else in the world. And of course you have never heard, for I have never told you, have I?' He smiled at her with such tenderness that she went pink and then quite pale. 'Is Adams now safely tucked up? Could he be left to his own devices for a little while?'

'Well, yes, I suppose so. But I have the sheets to put away. I said I would do that before I go.'

He held open the door without a word, waited while she made sure that the invalid had all he wanted, and ushered her out into the passage.

'The linen room,' directed Eloise, strangely short of breath, 'and really I can't think why you should want to see me.'

She was brought to a standstill by the simple expedient of having her waist clamped by his two hands and then turned round to face him. But she would look no higher than his chin. 'After all,' she reminded him, 'you walked off without...' Her voice became indignant at the very remembrance of it. 'You didn't even ask how I felt.' She glanced briefly up at his face, to encounter blue eyes which gleamed so brightly that she lowered her own in panic. 'Besides,' she went on, quite unable to stop herself now, 'when I left Holland you didn't m-mind—not in the least.'

'Did I say that, my Pineapple Girl?'

She said a little pettishly: 'No, you didn't, you just looked down your nose at me.'

'Shall I tell you what I really wanted to do?' His voice was full of laughter and something else, so that she said hastily and much against her inclination: 'No, I have to see to the sheets.'

He made no attempt to release her. 'Damn the sheets,' he observed mildly. 'I'm sure that Miss Maggs will be delighted to deal with them; I've not come all this way to watch you count linen.'

Eloise wriggled a little and his hands tightened. 'Well, why have you come?'

'To marry you, of course.'

Her eyes flew to his and this time she didn't lower them. 'Marry…?' she managed. 'But you've not asked me.' She added without conviction: 'Besides, I don't want to.'

He sighed loudly. 'My darling love, is that true? I do hope not, for I have the licence in my pocket and the parson waiting.'

'The parson…' Eloise's unremarkable features had assumed beauty as she assimilated this news; she felt a pleasant glow sweeping over her, but all the same she damped it down just for a moment. 'I'll not marry you until you explain about Liske. Besides, you let me go…'

He bent his head then and kissed her so that she really didn't care about his answer, but presently he said: 'I could hardly tell you that I loved you until I had made it quite clear to Liske that any feeling I had had for her was quite gone—and there never was much, you know, my dearest, and what little there was melted away when you fell in a heap at my feet and flung a pineapple at me.' He kissed her again. 'I told the Reverend Mr Culmer that we would be at the church by half past one.'

Eloise didn't know whether to laugh or cry. 'But it's long after twelve o'clock, and look at me...'

She shouldn't have said that, for he wasted quite a few minutes doing just that before observing: 'Very nice too, my darling, and something I shall never tire of doing.'

She gave his arm a little shake. 'Timon, darling Timon, you don't understand—I'm in uniform and I've got to pack and no one knows...it'll take ages to explain...'

'Don't fuss, woman.' He had stopped her by kissing her once more. 'I've already explained—why do you suppose I wanted to see Dr Dean in the first place? And you can change in ten minutes. If you can't pack in that time it really doesn't matter; we can stop somewhere and get what you need.'

She blinked at him, smiling gloriously. 'All right. You—you are sure, aren't you?' She wasn't given the chance to say more than that, though. Presently she said in a voice muffled by his shoulder: 'Will you tell me where we're to be married and where we're going?'

'In the village church, of course—I arranged that

yesterday. I was on the way to see the headmaster when I looked up and saw you. I've never been so frightened in all my life, dearest; to have found you and then to see you teetering wildly on the parapet far above my head.' His blue eyes searched hers. 'I died a dozen times before I reached you.' He pulled her closer and pulled the cap off her head. 'Such pretty hair. Once we're married we're going to drive over to Buttermere—they're expecting us at the inn there—we can have a late lunch.'

'Expecting us?' asked Eloise sharply. 'You were sure, weren't you?'

He answered her placidly. 'Yes, my darling, I was, just as you are sure—and we've wasted too much time already.'

'I'm sorry, Timon, of course I'm sure. I've loved you for—oh, ever since I first saw you, I suppose. Are we going to stay at Buttermere?'

'For a few days, then I'll take you to Eddles-combe before we go back to Holland.' He let her go reluctantly. 'Go and put on something pretty while I go and thank Miss Maggs. I'll wait for you there.'

She took rather less than the ten minutes Timon had given her; it was wonderful what one could do when one had a sufficiently good reason to do it. She was out of her uniform and into the green out-fit, and had her hair and face done, her velvet tammy nicely arranged, well within that period, and time to spare to search for her best gloves and handbag, urged on by her happiness and excitement.

The rest of her packing was done in a careless manner which would have revolted her normally, but now nothing was normal; it was a dream come true, so wonderful that she couldn't quite believe it.

The next few minutes were a confusion of good-byes and good wishes which she hardly heard; nor did she realise that she was in the car until they were driving away, out into the narrow road which led to the village. But the dream became glorious reality when they walked side by side up the churchyard path and Timon opened the old, creaking door and took her hand in his and kissed her very gently. 'This is where our life begins,' he said tenderly.

She kissed him back, for she had no words.

Harlequin Romance®

Delightful

Affectionate

Romantic

Emotional

Tender

Original

Daring

Riveting

Enchanting

Adventurous

Moving

Harlequin Romance—the
series that has it all!

HROM-G

HARLEQUIN 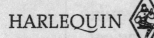 PRESENTS®

HARLEQUIN PRESENTS
men you won't be able to resist
falling in love with...

HARLEQUIN PRESENTS
women who have feelings
just like your own...

HARLEQUIN PRESENTS
powerful passion in
exotic international settings...

HARLEQUIN PRESENTS
intense, dramatic stories that will keep you
turning to the very last page...

HARLEQUIN PRESENTS
The world's bestselling romance series!

Harlequin® Historical

From rugged lawmen and
valiant knights to defiant heiresses
and spirited frontierswomen,
Harlequin Historicals will
capture your imagination with
their dramatic scope, passion
and adventure.

Harlequin Historicals...
they're too good to miss!